Murder in the Seventh Cavalry

BY

Robert Broomall

A BLUE STONE MEDIA PUBLICATION

Books by Robert Broomall

California Kingdoms
Texas Kingdoms
The Lawmen
The Bank Robber
Dead Man's Crossing (Jake Moran 1)
Dead Man's Town (Jake Moran 2)
Dead Man's Canyon (Jake Moran 3)
K Company (K Company 1)
Conroy's First Command (K Company 2)
The Dispatch Rider (K Company 3)
Scalp Hunters
Wild Bill and the Dinosaur Hunters

For James, Heather, and Diane

CHAPTER 1

1875

The three men were doing a good job of beating the hell out of me. Why not, they were professionals. I'd put up a fight, but at those odds it hadn't lasted long. Now I lay in the muddy alley, trying to cover up, while they stomped me.

I'd come to Cheyenne to do a job for the Union Pacific Railroad. During my stay I'd attracted the attention of a working girl named Suzy Hart, and by doing that I'd also attracted the attention of Three-Finger Jack Brannan, her pimp and lover. The job for the railroad was finished, and I'd been on my way to check the train schedules out of town when Brannan and his pals had jammed a pistol in my spine and hustled me off the street.

When they got bored kicking me, Brannan's two goons hauled me to my feet, holding my arms. It was early December. A chill wind blew rain that felt like it might turn to snow. The numbing cold made my pain a bit less intense. Three-Finger Jack stood in front of me, hatless and breathing hard from his exertions, his scraggly red beard pulled awry. With his good right hand he slugged me in the jaw, making my head snap back.

"This'll teach you to mess with Suzy," he said. "She ain't supposed to give it away for free."

I spat blood. "Maybe that's because I treated her like a lady."

Jack hit me again, and I sagged.

"I'm the only one gets it free," Jack said.

The two men who were holding me relaxed, thinking

1

that I was used up. I collected myself, then lashed up and out with the toe of my boot, catching Jack in the jaw and knocking him across the alley into the opposite wall.

Jack put his left hand, the one missing the fingers, to his cheek, which my kick had torn open. The rain washed blood through his beard down onto the front of his checked suit jacket. His porcine eyes flared with anger. "You son of a bitch, you could have left here alive. But not now. I'm goin' to take your head to Suzy in a box. I'm goin' to show her what happens when she gives it away for free. 'Course I'll have to tell her who you are, 'cause she ain't goin' to recognize you. Even that scar on your face will be gone when I'm done with you."

From his coat pocket, Jack drew a set of brass knuckles. He slipped them over the fingers of his right hand, taking his time, relishing the prospect of what was to come.

I kicked out again. Jack was expecting it this time and he jumped out of the way. "Hold him, damn you!" he told his shoulder hitters.

The two men gripped me more tightly. I struggled, throwing myself this way and that, but they got control of me, pinioning my legs with their own. One of the men, no-neck Dutch Emmerich, grabbed my hair and yanked back my head, holding it still.

Jack smiled; the stumps of his remaining teeth were mossy green. He took aim at my left eye and drew back his brass-knuckled fist.

I heard footsteps splash in the alley. A voice cried, "Hey!"

Jack turned. As he did, a two-by-four crashed into his face. Blood squirted, and he dropped onto his back like a pole-axed steer.

The two shoulder hitters let go of me and turned to face the newcomer, a big man in a tweed suit and bowler hat. Before they could do anything, he clobbered one of them, a gorilla named Natchez Mike, alongside the head with the two-by-four. Mike went down without a sound.

Dutch Emmerich tried to run, but I caught his arm, swung him around, and kicked him in the balls. Dutch bent over, clutching himself and retching. As he did, I grabbed his head and drove my knee into his face. He collapsed in the mud.

"Looks like I got here just in time," said my rescuer. He was about twenty-five, with sandy hair and moustache, and a stolid, almost ox-like countenance that belied the ferocity with which he had dispatched Jack Brannan.

I bent over the fallen men. Natchez Mike was out cold. Dutch wasn't going anywhere for a while without a truss. Pink froth bubbled around Jack's smashed face. "He's going to have a headache when he comes to," I told the newcomer. "If he comes to — it's been a long time since I've seen a man hit that hard. Come on — let's get out of here."

I got my hat. My rescuer tossed away the two-by-four, and we left the alley. I was bent over with pain and seeing double. My legs felt rubbery, like the bones had been pulled out of them. When we got to the street, I had to stop. I propped up a building, breathing hard, the cold rain running down my bruised, swollen face.

"Thanks," I told my new friend. "Lucky for me you happened along."

"It wasn't luck," the big man admitted. "I was looking for you."

"You were?" I straightened — cautiously, in case my

ribs were broken.

In that dim light I guess it was the first clear view the big man had of me, and he took an involuntary step back. I get that reaction a lot when people see the scar on my face. The scar runs from just under my left eye all the way to the corner of my jaw. It's ragged, to boot—Old Amos Bullock sewed it with the same needle and thread he used for mending his buckskins, and he wasn't real handy with them.

The big man recovered, clearing his throat. "That's right. I asked for you at the hotel, and the clerk told me you'd just left. I saw you way up the street—there was hardly anyone else out—and I started after you. But before I got very far, you were dragged off by those three men. So I looked for a weapon. Fortunately somebody left that lumber lying around." Then something occurred to him. Almost apologetically, he said, "I did get the right man, didn't I? You are Lysander Hughes? The detective?"

"That's right."

"I'm Jim Calhoun." He handed me his card. It read:

"James E. Calhoun
First Lieutenant
Seventh U.S. Cavalry"

"The Seventh," I said, raising my brows. "Custer's outfit."

"Yes." Calhoun couldn't help but smile, revealing his pride in that elite unit.

"Well, what do you want with me, Lieutenant?"

"It's not me that wants you, actually. It's the General. He wants to hire you."

CHAPTER 2

There weren't a lot of people on the street in this weather, but I was the only one who looked like he'd been on the business end of a bucking bronc, and the few passersby were beginning to stare. "Let's get out of here," I told Lieutenant Calhoun, "before somebody finds those three in the alley, and we have some explaining to do."

We headed back to my hotel, the Metropole, with the icy rain battering our faces and the wind blowing trash down the street like yesterday's memories. At least the bad weather masked the smells of excrement and urine and butchered animals left to rot that usually hung over towns like Cheyenne. It wasn't dark yet, but lamps were lit in most of the buildings, dim yellow pools in the wet. Behind us, there were cries. I looked back and saw a uniformed policeman running down the street.

Entering the hotel, I led Calhoun up the stairs to my room. Despite the hotel's fancy name, the room wasn't much—there was a rickety bed with a straw mattress, a chair with uneven legs, a battered dresser and porcelain washstand. The place might have been swept once, but I couldn't prove it.

I lit the lamp and trimmed it, pointing to the chair. "Have a seat," I told Calhoun. "Drink?"

"Thanks," he said.

I kept a bottle of Napoleon brandy on the dresser, a ring underneath showing where it had been set down wet. I blew dust out of a glass and poured a couple fingers worth for the lieutenant. Then I tilted the bottle back, and I drank until I felt a comforting numbness massage the pounding edges of my pain.

Calhoun reversed the chair as he sat, resting his forearms on its back. Gingerly, wincing, I lowered myself onto the edge of the bed. Rain rattled the dirty windowpane as Calhoun stared at my face. "That's a nasty scar, Mr. Hughes. May I ask how you got it?"

"Comanche war axe," I told him. "Back in '58. On the Canadian River, with Rip Ford and the Texas Rangers, when we killed Chief Iron Shirt. Lucky I was pulling away at the time, or it would have caved in my face."

Calhoun's blue eyes widened with astonishment. "'Fifty-eight? That was . . . seventeen years ago. You must have been awfully young."

"I was sixteen," I said. "Old enough."

"I envy you. I'm twenty-five, and I haven't seen a real battle yet."

"I'd be happy to trade you a few of mine."

"Will you tell me about this Iron Shirt character some time?"

"What there is to tell," I said. "But right now, why don't you tell me why General Custer wants to hire me."

Calhoun stared into his glass. "Three days ago, on December Sixth, one of our officers, Lieutenant Peter Redington of I Company, was murdered at Fort Abraham Lincoln, Dakota Territory. He was killed by his own men."

I whistled. A murder in the country's top military unit. Enlisted men killed each other all the time, but an officer? "How'd it happen?"

"One of the guards found him, at dawn, just outside the post boundary. We'd had a cold snap, with the bulb below zero and high winds. The guard, Private Stella, saw a man apparently sitting on the ground. He approached and challenged, but got no answer. Moving closer, he saw that the man was wearing nothing but his underwear. He had been bucked and gagged. That's an army punishment."

"I know what it is," I said. A man was placed on the ground, and his hands were tied beneath his legs so that he couldn't move. The practice was officially outlawed, but a lot of outfits still used it.

Calhoun went on. "Private Stella says he thought it must be a man set out for punishment, though why in that weather and why outside post bounds he couldn't figure. Then he realized who it was, and he tried to help him. But by then, it was too late. Lieutenant Redington had frozen to death. He'd been beaten as well."

"No one saw anything?"

"No." Calhoun took a drink of his brandy. He looked shaken. Being murdered by your own men probably wasn't on the course of instruction at West Point. "Redington was popular, with a good career in front of him. The General wants a detective to go into I Company and learn the identity of the killer, or killers."

"Why a detective? Doesn't the army have official ways of learning these things? A board of inquiry or something?"

Calhoun shook his head. "Enlisted men will stick together against the officers. They won't betray one of their own. And the few who might talk are afraid. It's a rough bunch we're dealing with—the company is known as 'Wild I.' It'll take another enlisted man to gain their confidence.

"Besides," he went on, "a board of inquiry would

7

create scandal, for the General and the regiment. You can imagine what the press would do with that—we've had a hard time hushing it up the incident as it is. There's a big campaign being planned against the Sioux and Cheyenne next spring, and the Seventh is going to be part of it. It may bring the last great Indian battle on this continent. A lot of unfortunate publicity and legal maneuvering could jeopardize the regiment's place in that battle."

I rose and refilled Calhoun's glass, then took another long drink from the bottle. The brandy's warmth felt good in the chill room. "Why pick me? Why not go to one of the big agencies, like the Pinkertons?"

"It was Mrs. Custer's idea. She's good friends with the scout Hickok—Wild Bill. She wired him for advice, and he recommended you. He gave us your address in San Francisco, and your forwarding service told us where to find you."

I nodded. I'd tangled with Hickok during the war, when we had fought on different sides; later, I'd saved his bacon in Abilene when he was marshal there. Custer hated Hickok, though—because of some trouble Hickok had with Custer's brother Tom in Hays City—so Hickok's recommendation wasn't likely to make the Boy General, or Tom, all that well disposed towards me. I wondered why Custer had gone along with his wife's idea.

"How can you be certain that Redington was killed by his men?" I asked.

"Who else could it have been?" Calhoun said. "The method—bucking and gagging—suggests it was some trooper's bad idea of a joke."

"Unless that's the way it was meant to seem. Why would his men want to kill him?"

"I can't imagine. He only joined the regiment in July.

He hadn't been with us long enough to make any enemies."

"Looks like he made one, at least. What about the fellow who found the body — Stella? Do you think he was part of it?"

"I don't know. Captain Keogh — I's commander — will fill you in on that."

"You're not in I Company?"

"No."

I peered out the rain-streaked window. There was a hubbub down Eddy Street where Jack Brannan had been poleaxed, but nobody seemed to be looking for us. Brannan's death — if he was dead — wasn't the kind of crime likely to trouble the police long. We'd done them a favor. "When was Lieutenant Redington last seen alive?"

"About eleven-thirty, at the Officers Club. He'd been playing pool with Lieutenant Manley of the Twentieth Infantry and Captain Yates of A Company. He left for his quarters."

"Had he been drinking?"

"Drinking, but not drunk, as I understand it."

"You weren't there?"

"No."

"Did he have enemies among the officers or civilians on the post?"

"No. Like I said, he was quite popular, especially as he was such a fresh face." Calhoun brushed back his unruly thatch of blond hair and stared at me earnestly. "Will you take the assignment?"

"My fee is a hundred dollars down, plus ten dollars a day."

"That's a lot."

"It's my fee. Take it or leave it."

"Army officers—even senior officers like the General—don't make much money, you know."

"I'm aware of that."

Calhoun seemed unsure what to do. "The General authorized me to agree to anything within reason. I guess this is within reason. I have just enough cash with me to cover the advance. So—will you do it?"

I considered. I wasn't thrilled with the idea of joining the army, even for a short while—I'd seen enough of armies to last me. I liked young Calhoun, though. He'd saved my life in that alley, and I owed him. And I was intrigued with the idea of meeting Custer, who was, after all, one of the most famous men in America. Besides, I needed the money—everything I'd earned from the U.P. had gone to pay off debts incurred on my last trip into Texas searching for my lost sister Becky. If I was going to make another trip next year, I'd need money to finance it.

"I'll do it," I said.

"Good." From a pocket of his jacket Calhoun produced a billfold and counted out a hundred dollars in greenbacks. "I hope you're a fast worker. I'll get skinned if you aren't."

I grinned at him. "In that case, I'll work as fast as I can."

I prepared and signed a receipt for the money. I also drew up a document that would get me released from the army in case something went wrong. After he had signed my paper, Calhoun said, "Present yourself at the adjutant's office to enlist. Lieutenant Cooke, the regimental adjutant, knows you're coming. He'll see that you're posted to I. Will you be using your own name?"

"I suppose. I doubt anybody in the Seventh knows me. How many others are aware that you're hiring a detective?"

"Well, there's the General and Mrs. Custer, of course. And Tom. Captain Keogh. I guess they'll tell Lieutenant Porter, too—he's I Company's other—"

"No. Too many know already, for my liking. No one else is to be let in on the plan."

"All right, I'll inform the General. When can you leave?"

"Tonight. I'll take the train to Omaha, then go by steamboat to Bismarck."

Calhoun brightened. "We can travel together then."

"No," I said. "From this moment, we don't know each other."

"Is that necessary?"

"Maybe not, but I've found that the fewer chances I take, the longer I live. I'll see you at Fort Lincoln."

"Actually, you won't. I'm stationed at Fort Rice, downriver from Lincoln."

"Fort Rice?" I said. "Tell me something. If you're not in I Company, and you're not at Lincoln, how do you know so much about this affair, and how did you get the job of coming after me?"

"I guess you could say I'm part of the General's inner circle," Calhoun said, and he grinned sheepishly. "I married his sister."

"How many relatives does the General have working for him, anyway?"

"Just me and Tom, right now—Tom's captain of C Troop. Their brother Boston and a nephew are coming out to join us for the spring campaign."

"I never realized the Seventh was a family enterprise," I said. I put down the bottle. I'd killed a lot of the pain from my beating, but it would be back, like a bad debt. "I hate to cut this short, Lieutenant, but if you'll excuse me, I've got a lot to do if I'm going to be on a train this evening."

"I understand," Calhoun said. He shook my hand. "I still want you to tell me about the Rangers and Chief Iron Shirt."

"I will," I said. "I promise."

"That's a promise I'll hold you to."

"Good. Oh, and tell Captain Keogh I'll need a list of I Company's men who were on guard the night Redington was killed."

"All right." Calhoun shuffled his feet. "Well . . . goodbye, for now. And thanks." He put down his glass and left the room. From the window I watched him emerge onto the rainy street, a brawny young man in a tweed suit and bowler hat, full of promise.

Seven months later, he was dead. I've often wondered if, in those last moments, he thought about the Texas Rangers and Chief Iron Shirt.

CHAPTER 3

Fort Abraham Lincoln lay at the foot of a bluff overlooking the Missouri River. It was not like an easterner's idea of a fort. There was no stockade or gates, just frame buildings sprawled across the plain — though there were three wooden blockhouses facing west, where sentries could watch for marauding Indians. The original post, built for infantry, had been on top of the bluff, but was now abandoned.

I approached the fort's main entrance, which was flanked by a guard in light blue overcoat, white gloves and forage cap. I had changed my appearance since leaving Cheyenne. I now looked like a man down on his luck, wearing second-hand clothes and a moth-eaten mackinaw that I'd picked up in Omaha. I had taken the steamer *Far West* to Bismarck, an unremarkable oasis of raw wood and whiskey in a sea of mud. I had crossed the river by ferry and tramped three miles through the clinging goo to Fort Lincoln. It was a bitter, windy day, and I was splashed with mud by wagons and riders, adding to my cultivated air of seediness.

Fort Lincoln was laid out in the form of a square, with the parade ground in the center. On the western side of the square were the officers' quarters; directly across from them were the enlisted men's barracks. The other two sides of the square were occupied with buildings necessary for running the post. Everything was marked off by rows of whitewashed rocks. Behind the parade

13

ground square were the stables, Suds Row — where the laundresses and married enlisted personnel lived — the teamsters' quarters, and various huts and teepees belonging to the scouts. On the plain west of the fort a company of cavalry was drilling. Everywhere there were soldiers working — painting, hammering, digging, hauling. There were the smells of horses, burning firewood, and bread from the bake house, along with the nose-wrenching mixture of quicklime, excrement, and urine so peculiar to army latrines. Somewhere dogs were barking.

Following the guard's direction, I came to a frame building on the north end of the parade ground with a neatly lettered sign saying "Adjutant" in front. I mounted the porch, went in, and found myself in an anteroom, where a uniformed clerk sat at a desk, copying orders. The clerk glanced up at me. Before he could say anything, there were voices, and an officer ushered a young lady from the back room. The officer, a lieutenant whom I assumed to be the adjutant, Cooke, sported an enormous set of sidewhiskers, called dundrearies, which came halfway down his chest. He guided the lady by the arm.

"I've told you before, Miss Winslow, Lieutenant Redington died of natural causes. There's no story for you here. There's nothing for you, or your paper, to investigate. The situation is tragic enough without you trying to make it something that it's not. Now if you would please — "

"That's not what I hear," Miss Winslow said. She was above average height and radiated self-confidence, with dark red hair tied in a bun. Her relatively mud-free shoes and dress showed that she must have caught a ride from the ferry in the post ambulance.

14

"And where do you hear these things?" asked the lieutenant.

Miss Winslow smiled coyly. "Lieutenant Cooke, you know I can't tell you that."

Cooke drew himself up, he was lean, with the easy grace of an athlete. "I know two things, Miss Winslow — one is that women shouldn't be journalists. The other is that you so-called journalists never show up unless you think there's something bad for you to write about. You never tell about the good things the army does. You never write about the sacrifices these boys make, the hardships they endure to make people like you safe. Your only goal is to expose them to the world as baby killers and rapists. Now, if you'll excuse me, I have my duties to perform."

"Can't I just speak to — ?"

"No, you may not. And if you don't leave the post this minute, I'll have you arrested. There are no separate facilities for women in our guardhouse, so you might find that experience rather to your distaste."

The young woman hesitated. Cooke turned to the clerk. "Barrett, call the guard."

"Yes, sir," said the private, rising.

"All right," said Miss Winslow, raising a hand in surrender. "I'll go — for now."

Cooke went on. "You should comport yourself with more dignity, Miss Winslow. If your goal is, as you say, to become a war correspondent," — behind the lieutenant, the clerk snorted a laugh — "making enemies with the army is not the way to go about it. We would, after all, be the ones responsible for ensuring that that lovely red hair remained on your head and not on Sitting Bull's coup stick. Or perhaps he would simply add you to his list of wives."

Miss Winslow's full lips narrowed with anger, and she turned on her heel. As she did, she noticed me. Our eyes met. Then she left. I watched her go, wondering who she was and what she knew about Redington's death — and how she knew it.

As Lieutenant Cooke returned to his office, his clerk said to me, "Can I help you?"

"I'm looking to join up," I told him.

The clerk stared at me a moment, then stuck his head in the office next to Cooke's. "Sergeant Major Sharrow, there's a tramp here says he wants to enlist."

The august person who entered the anteroom looked like a recruiting officer's fantasy — anvil chest, immaculate uniform, sandy moustache waxed at the ends. You didn't need to see the stripes piled on his sleeves to know that this was the regimental sergeant major. He looked me up and down, as a scientist might study an inferior life form, which I probably seemed to him — I was unshaven, hadn't washed in days, and my mud-splattered clothes were ready for the rag pile. He spoke with an Irish lilt. "What's yer name, then?"

"Lysander Hughes."

At the mention of my name, a chair scraped, and Lieutenant Cooke appeared behind the sergeant major. Cooke's blue eyes met mine.

Sharrow went on. "Lysander? Whit the divil kind o' name is that?"

"Lysander was a Spartan admiral who defeated the Athenians," I explained, adding, "My father had a classical turn of mind."

Sharrow's beefy face was blank. He probably didn't know Sparta from Timbuktu. "And why would a classical fellow like yerself be wantin' to join the army? Hard times

16

I'm guessin', by yer look."

"That's true," I admitted. "I had a ranch in Nebraska, but it went bust, and I can't get work."

"Enlistment's five years. Pay's thirteen dollars a month, payable whiniver Uncle Sam sees fit to send it — which ain't often."

"I can live with that."

"Have ye served with the colors before?"

"No."

"How old are ye?"

"Thirty-three."

"That's under the limit, but not by much. Soldiering's a young man's game, Hughes. Why should we take you?"

"Because I can ride and I can shoot."

Sharrow and the lieutenant exchanged glances. "Sure, and we don't get many like that," Sharrow muttered.

Lieutenant Cooke took up the questioning. "You talk like a Reb, Hughes. Where are you from?"

"Texas."

"Fight in the war?"

"Some." I'd spent most of my wartime service as a spy, but I didn't mention that. "I fought Indians with the Texas Rangers."

Sergeant Major Sharrow eyed the scar on my cheek, and the bruises which remained from my beating at the hands of Jack Brannan and his pals. "Ye've the look of a jailbird about ye. Sure ye're not runnin' from the law?"

"I'm sure," I said — which was something of a lie, since I was wanted for murder in Texas.

"Bit of a scrapper, though, eh?"

I shrugged.

Sharrow growled, uncertain about me. Lieutenant Cooke decided for him. "Normally we take just about any able-bodied man who wants to sign up, Hughes. Just now we can afford to be choosy. We recently received a hundred and fifty recruits from the depot at Jefferson Barracks—only sixty with prior service, I'm sorry to say. The ten companies here in Dakota have their full complements. We've lost two of the recruits, though. One got kicked in the head by his horse and died, the other died from fever. Despite your age, you seem to possess some unique qualifications, so we'll take you if you pass the physical."

The clerk, Barrett, was ordered to take me to the post hospital, where the contract surgeon, Dr. Lord, a stoop-shouldered, dyspeptic New Englander, gave me the physical.

"Take off your clothes," he instructed.

I undressed, revealing an assortment of scars from bullets, arrows, knives, and what have you. Barrett and DeWolf, the assistant surgeon, whistled at the sight. Dr. Lord said, "You seem to have led an interesting life, Mr. Hughes."

"That's one word for it," I told him.

The doctor directed me to the scale. He called off the readings while his orderly noted them on my papers. "Height—six foot, even. Weight—one seventy-one." He pried open my mouth as though he were inspecting a horse, then thumped my back and chest. "No obvious defects. Quite an impressive physical specimen, in fact, not like most of the ones we get. You'll do."

I took my paperwork back to the adjutant's office, where Sharrow looked it over. "Where shall we put him, sir?" he asked the adjutant. "D Company?"

"No," said Cooke, and there was a twinkle in his eyes as they met mine again. "Try I. Let's see what Myles

Keogh and Frank Varden can make of him."

"Very well, sir."

I signed the enlistment papers, and Lieutenant Cooke administered the oath of allegiance. "Congratulations," he said, when I finished.

"Thanks," I replied.

At that, Sharrow whacked the side of my head with his open hand, making me see stars. "Say 'sir' when ye speak to an officer. Ye're in the army, now." To the clerk, he said, "Barrett, march this sorry excuse for a soldier to the quartermaster and see he's issued his gear. Then take him to the bathhouse and get him cleaned up."

CHAPTER 4

After I'd had a bath and a shave, the headquarters clerk, Barrett, took me to the Quartermaster store, where the duty sergeant loaded me down with clothing and equipment. I was issued an ill-fitting blue coat, light blue trousers and ankle-high shoes that felt more like cardboard than leather. A caped overcoat and forage cap completed my attire. The rest of the gear I stuffed into a blue denim duffel bag, then Barrett turned me over to I Company's first sergeant, Varden, who had been called away from stable duty.

Varden was a banty rooster of a man, with a square head and bristly moustache, who bounced around on the balls of his feet like a boxer. He looked me up and down while I stood at what I hoped was attention.

"You talk like sesesh, Hughes, and I don't like sesesh. That means I don't like you. You got the look of trouble. Well, get one thing straight. I've been in this man's army since Eighteen and Fifty-four. I got scars on my back from being flogged, I got disjointed thumbs from bein' hung up by 'em. During the war I captained a company of volunteers. I know every trick there is in the book, and a few the book ain't heard about. Do what you're told, when you're told to do it, and we'll get along. Don't—and I'll make you wish you'd never been born. Do we understand each other?"

"Yes."

"Say, 'Yes, First Sergeant' when you speak to me."

"Yes, First Sergeant."

"All right, move out. Follow me."

He marched me to the post trader's store. The front room was fitted out as a general store, while there was a bar and pool table in the back. The store was doing a brisk business, military and civilian. The trader ran a wagon service from the ferry to the fort, so that townspeople could shop there—the prices must be better than those in Bismarck.

Sergeant Varden ignored the busy clerk and knocked on the office door. "Mr. Haselmere?" he cried.

The door opened and a stocky, heavy-jowled fellow emerged. He wore a flashy cravat with an enormous stickpin, and his brilliantined hair gleamed even in the weak December light. Behind him, in the office, I glimpsed a pair of teamsters. One wore a red bandanna on his head; the other had a gray streak, white almost, down the middle of his beard.

Haselmere shut the office door quickly, as if he didn't want anyone to see the teamsters. "What can I do for you, Sergeant?"

"Recruit needs a cleaning kit," Varden said.

"Coming up," said Haselmere.

He went to the back shelves and returned with a pre-packaged box of polishes, brushes and cleaning cloths, which he placed on the varnished counter. "That's three dollars, soldier—to be withheld from your first pay." He got out a tally book. "What's your name?"

I poked through the box. "Looks like a lot of stuff I don't need in here—not for near a quarter of a month's pay, I don't. There's enough polish to outfit a bootblack's stand."

"It's what everybody gets," Sergeant Varden said

sharply, and I wondered how much of a kickback he received on each sale.

"What's your name?" Haselmere repeated.

"Hughes," I told him. "Lysander."

"How do you spell 'Lysander?' "

"With an 'L.' "

"Hard case—are you, Hughes?" said Sergeant Varden. "Well, we'll soon take that out of you. Pack that kit and fall in."

I crammed the cleaning kit into the already bulging duffel bag. Under his dark moustache, Haselmere smiled smugly. "So long, soldier. I'll look forward to your business."

"At the prices you charge, I don't doubt it," I told him. "Beats robbing stagecoaches for a living."

Varden shoved me through the door. Outside, he barked, "Stand at attention, you sesesh sack of shit!"

I complied.

Varden braced himself, hands on hips, and thrust his mug up into mine, so close I could smell the cheap tobacco on his breath. "I don't know why you joined this outfit, Hughes, but I know you won't make a soldier. You've got a bad attitude, and you're too old." (I was getting damned tired of people telling me how old I was.) "Attitude I can fix, but age I can't. So I'm going to run you out early, make you desert, and save Uncle Sam his thirteen dollars a month. Hoist that bag over your head."

I did.

"Now, double time!"

I started running. Varden ran beside me, his reddening face still thrust at mine, chanting in a singsong voice. "Hut, hut. Your left, your left, your left, right, left. You're out of step, you Texas turd. Don't you know your right from your left?"

"Of course I do," I snapped.

He stuck out a foot and tripped me. I fell in the mud, with the bag in front of me. "Say 'Yes, First Sergeant' when you speak to me. Let me hear it!"

"Yes, First Sergeant."

"What are you doing on the ground? Get up! Hoist that bag! Double time! Your left, your left, your left, right, left."

CHAPTER 5

We took the long way to the barracks, running once around the parade ground, with me holding the heavy duffel bag over my head and Sergeant Varden calling cadence. Despite the cold, I was sweating plenty beneath my overcoat, and my shoulders burned by the time we got to I Company's barracks.

"Halt!" ordered Varden. "Fall out."

The frame barracks was built in the shape of a "T," with the crossbar facing the parade ground. A passageway ran from the front door down the center of the crossbar, leading to the mess hall and kitchen. On each side of the passage were troop bays with rows of bunks—mattresses folded neatly on top of them, wooden lockers at their feet. Shelves and pegs ran around the room, holding additional clothing and items of equipment. At the end of each bay were carbine and pistol racks, along with a cast-iron stove. The bays smelled of varnish and gun oil. Men, most of them hard looking and lean as wolves, lounged inside, removing their white stable outfits, waiting for mess call. They looked up as we came in.

"Sergeant Morgan!" said Varden.

A mournful-faced fellow with slicked-down, thinning hair detached himself from a little group. "Yeah, Top?"

"This recruit is for your platoon, Second Squad. His name is Hughes." Varden turned to me. "Remember, Hughes, I've got my eye on you."

As the first sergeant retreated to his cubicle at one end of the bay, Sergeant Morgan said, "Glad to have you, Hughes."

"Thanks," I replied.

Over his shoulder, Morgan cried, "Peaches!"

An olive-complexioned young man with a long nose and bad haircut came forward. "What is it, Sarge?" He spoke with a heavy Italian accent.

"This is Hughes. He'll be your new bunky. Hughes, this is Private Stella."

We nodded to each other. Stella was the man who had found Lieutenant Redington's body. He had a good natured, open face, the kind of man you'd pass in the street and take no notice of, the kind of fellow you'd want for a neighbor—if you wanted neighbors. He didn't look like a killer, but neither did a lot of the killers I'd met.

To me, Sergeant Morgan said, "You and Peaches will share your blankets and shelter halves in the field. You'll mess together, march together, fight together. Most of what you need to know about soldiering you'll learn from him and the other men in your group of four. Right now, Peaches will help you get your bedding and get your gear squared away."

Peaches showed me to an empty bunk, where I dropped the duffel bag. He introduced me to the others in our group of four—a dreamy-eyed, angular Midwesterner called Two-Bit; and a square-jawed, almost too handsome fellow called Dick Daring. I was aware of the other men in the barracks watching me. One jug-eared fellow, a brawler by his look, showed particular interest.

Next, Peaches took me back to the Quartermaster's to draw my bedding. "You are lucky to get in this platoon," he said, his breath frosting on the chill air. "Sergeant

Morgan, he is a good man. Sergeant Bustard in First Platoon, he is very hard."

"Why do they call you Peaches?" I asked him.

"My name, it is Antonio, but on the payday, I always buy the tinned peaches at the trader store, so—it is 'Peaches.' "

"Where you from?"

"The Calabrese. In *Italia*. A village called Santa Vittoria."

"What brings you to the States?"

"In Santa Vittoria I am apprentice to a carpenter. But there is no future for me there. I want to go to America — to be rich, and have the big house. But when I get here, I realize --" he hit himself in the head to indicate stupidity— "I do not speak the English. I cannot get job. So—I join the army to learn. It is hard for me at first, but now I say 'God damn' and 'cock-suck,'—just like real American." He grinned proudly.

At the Quartermaster's, I was issued two blankets and a mattress which I filled with clean straw at the stables. Peaches carried the blankets for me as we walked back.

"When I was up at the adjutant's, enlisting, they were talking about some dead lieutenant," I mentioned. "I think they said you were the one that found him."

Peaches halted, blanching. "They think I kill him?"

"I don't know. Did you?"

"No! Never!"

"Who did?"

He hesitated. "I don' know."

"They were going on about how it happened in front of your post, or something like that. I guess that's what's got them suspicious—how you didn't see anything."

"But I could not see!"

26

"Why?"

"I was not—please, do not tell this to anyone—I was not at my post."

"Where were you?"

"In the blockhouse. Because of the cold. You are not in the wind there. The Officer of Day, he has made rounds. I do not think there is much—how you say it?—danger for being catched."

"Don't they shoot you for that sort of thing?"

"Si—yes, they can—but they never do. It happen too much. They give you time in the mill—the guardhouse—or maybe they hang you by the thumb. Still, it is better than to freeze."

"So how did you find this lieutenant's body?"

"I see it at dawn. I have come back on sentry at six. Before, is too dark to see. The body, it is too far out. But I do not kill him."

"You're sure that somebody killed him? I mean, he didn't get drunk, pass out, and freeze to death?"

"Not unless he tie himself up first. Hit himself in head."

Back in the barracks, Peaches showed me the army way to fold my mattress on the bunk—mattresses weren't allowed to be unfolded till just before Lights Out. The jug-eared brawler was watching me again, standing with a bunch of his pals. A triangle began tinging from the passageway.

"Mess call," Peaches said.

As we started for the mess hall, the brawler blocked my path. "Hey, Pretty Boy, that's a nice scar on your face. How'd you get it?"

"Cut myself shaving." I pushed past him and followed Peaches into the mess hall.

On the serving line, the kitchen helpers gave each man a slice of cold beef, a piece of bread, and a cup of coffee. I joined the rest of my platoon at a long table, furnished with salt, brown sugar, bottles of vinegar and molasses. There was iron flatware with crossed sabers and "I - 7" on the handles. The sergeants had their own table; the corporals ate with the men.

I doctored the beef with vinegar and molasses, then folded it between the bread. Now I knew why the men were so lean. "You boys sure know how to tie on the feed bag," I commented.

"You'll get used to it," laughed Dick Daring. "This is all we ever have. Beef, bread, and coffee for breakfast; beef, bread, and coffee for dinner; beef, bread, and coffee for supper."

"Play fair now," admonished Two-Bit in his flat, Midwestern drawl. "Sometimes they give us beef hash for breakfast."

"This is better'n some posts I been at," grunted a white-haired, older fellow down the table. "I seen places where all you get is salt pork and hardtack, three times a day. Hell, I seen rocks invoiced as food. Least we got beef."

"Haselmere, the post trader, supplies it," explained Dick Daring. "Gives the cooks such a good price, they wouldn't think of having anything else."

"What's the outfit like?" I asked.

"If you mean the regiment, it's shit," said Dick Daring, sawing at his meat.

I was surprised. "This is supposed to be the best regiment in the army."

There were hoots of laughter. Dick Daring said, "A good regiment cares about its men. We could all die tomorrow and it wouldn't bother Hard Ass."

"Hard Ass?" I said.

"Custer."

"Cuss-turd," another fellow repronounced it.

"Custer's supposed to be a great general," I said. "Thought you boys idolized him."

More derisive laughter. "That prick?" said the white-haired fellow. "He couldn't general his way out of a Mexican whorehouse."

"Or into one," said somebody else.

"All he cares about is the newspapers, with his name in them," said a moon-faced young German.

Dick Daring said, "Custer's the type who takes all the credit when things go right, and none of the blame when they go wrong."

"Well," I said, "that takes care of the regiment. How about the company? I hear you all killed one of your officers."

The table fell silent.

"Where'd you hear that?" asked the white-haired man, looking at me with narrowed eyes.

"They were talking about it at Headquarters when I was there. What did you all do to him?"

The jug-eared brawler set down his coffee cup with a thump. "You ask a lot of questions, Pretty Boy."

"Just want to know what I'm getting into, is all. It's no skin off me, you want to kill your officers. We did it all the time in Texas."

"Maybe you didn't hear me," said the brawler. "Mind your own business."

I looked him in the eye. "Who are you?"

"Name's Doyle. My friends call me Bucko."

"There can't be many of those, so what do the rest of

us call you?"

Doyle's pals found this crack pretty funny, but Doyle steamed. "You got a big mouth, Pretty Boy."

"Part of my charm," I told him.

I rose from the table and left the mess hall. I figured somebody in the company would take a run at me, as the new man, and I guessed it was going to be this Doyle character. I wanted to be sure that when it happened, it was on my terms.

As the men finished supper, they drifted back into the barracks to put on their dress uniforms and get ready for evening parade. I was excused parade until I'd had some training, so I sat on my footlocker, unclasped the heart-shaped locket from my neck, and began to shine it with polish from my kit. The locket was made from cheap brass, the kind that turns your skin green when it hasn't been cleaned for a while, and this one hadn't been.

"Hey—lookee here, boys." It was Bucko Doyle, looming over me. "Pretty Boy's got hisself a locket. Ain't that cute?"

There was laughter around the bay.

I kept polishing.

Doyle went on in a mocking voice. "Got a picture in there, Pretty Boy? Who is it—your girl? Your mommy?"

I kept polishing.

Doyle reached for the locket. "Let me see."

I spoke in a low, even voice. "Touch that locket, and I'll kill you."

I stood. The barracks went quiet.

Doyle's close-set eyes narrowed with disbelief. "What did you say?"

"You heard me." I tossed the locket on my folded blankets. "There it is, take it—if you've got the guts."

"You piece of shit, I'll kick your face in. I'll make you eat that locket."

I gave him a slow smile. "You need to relax more, Doyle. Why don't you do your sister? She probably won't even charge you, you being family and all."

Doyle's eyes lit up and he roared at me, as I'd intended. A right uppercut to the point of his nose staggered him, drawing blood. A left and right to the jaw put him down. I kicked him hard in the ribs, drawing a gasp of pain. I got ready to do it again.

I was pulled away. "That's enough!" said Sergeant Varden.

Doyle lay on the floor, holding his ribs. "Doyle, get ready for parade," Varden told him. "And be quick — 'Trumpeters Assembly' is in five minutes." He turned to me. "Damn it, Hughes, I knew you'd be trouble."

Doyle wiped blood from his nose. I offered him a hand up, but he pushed it away and got up on his own.

"This ain't over," he said. "Not by a long shot."

CHAPTER 6

The evening parade was signaled by a flourish from the massed trumpeters, then the regimental band played "Garry Owen," the Seventh Cavalry's marching song. Five companies, all of the regiment that was stationed at Fort Lincoln, marched out, guidons snapping in the breeze, each company mounted on matching color horses. The men wore black spiked helmets with yellow horsehair plumes, modeled on those used by the Prussian army. Though it was freezing cold, they wore no overcoats so that their dark blue jackets with the fancy yellow facings would show.

I Company was second in line, on black horses, led by Captain Keogh, who cut a dashing pose with black moustache and imperial, on his horse Comanche. But the column was dominated by the lithe, graceful figure at its head, mounted on a high-stepping chestnut—George Armstrong Custer, the Boy General. The officers' wives watched the parade from the porch of Custer's huge house. A smattering of civilians and tame Indians clustered around the edges of the parade ground.

The companies formed on the parade ground, facing Custer and his staff. Cooke, the Adjutant, took the roll call and read the day's standing orders. Then Custer trotted his horse in front of the command. He halted, waiting, drawing all eyes upon him, making sure he was the center of attention. He was a showman, was Custer; the only man I ever saw who could make a flourish out of doing nothing. At last he shouted, "Draw sabers!"

There was a rasp of metal, and two hundred sabers flashed in the dying light. The band started playing again. Led by Custer, the five companies marched around the parade ground. Bugles blared; Custer shouted more orders, which were repeated by the company officers and sergeants. The troops swung from column of fours into column of platoons, then column of companies. All the while the band played martial airs, and the women on Custer's porch tapped their feet or drummed their fingers in time: "John Brown's Body," "Marching Through Georgia," and "Garry Owen" — always "Garry Owen."

"Cap'n Keogh gave the regiment 'Garry Owen,' you know," said Farrell, one of the cook's helpers who had joined me on the barracks porch. "New meat like you had best learn the words. Cap'n don't like it if you don't know the words."

Now the regiment formed line, wheeled left, then right in perfect alignment, then trotted across the parade ground in a mock charge before reforming into column of tours again. It was a spectacle of American precision and power out here on the dreary edge of eternity.

That night I lay in my bunk as the mournful notes of "Taps" floated across the parade ground. I drifted off to sleep, listening to the distant sounds of music and laughter from Officers Row.

* * *

Something was thrown over my head. Wool. A blanket. I couldn't breathe. I tried to get up, but something hard hit me in the face. I was hit again, then again and again and again, a rain of blows. I was powerless to resist. Stars exploded before my eyes.

There were shouts, a scurrying of feet.

The blanket was drawn from my face, my skin sticking to it, wet with blood. I felt no pain; that would come later. A hurricane lamp glowed. Figures swam in and out of focus. Voices sounded like they were coming from under water.

"God damn," breathed Peaches, looking down at me.

Dick Daring was sickened. "You're lucky you weren't killed."

"What'd they hit him with?" said Two-Bit.

"Some kind of cosh, it looks like," Dick said.

They didn't have to ask who had done it. Everyone in the barracks knew — and no one knew. There had been no witnesses; the perpetrator was safely back in his bunk.

I could almost hear him laughing.

CHAPTER 7

I made a hell of a sight at roll call next morning—my face was the color of an overripe plum, crusted with dried blood, lumpy as day-old mashed potatoes.

Sergeant Varden could scarcely conceal his amusement. "What happened to you, Hughes?"

"Fell out of bed, First Sergeant."

"Better be more careful—you might hurt yourself next time."

I didn't have to look to see the grins on the faces of Doyle and his friends.

After morning fatigue, Sergeant Morgan marched me back to the Quartermaster's, where I was issued a single-shot Springfield carbine and a .45 Colt's pistol. "I'd let this business with Doyle drop," the mournful-faced sergeant said as we returned to the company area. "Call it even and forget it. Doyle's a bad man to have against you."

"So am I," I told him.

"In case you missed what I said, Hughes, that's an order. I got enough trouble on my hands just now—what with all these new men and a big campaign coming. I just want to finish out my hitch, marry my girl, and settle down. I don't need no more problems. Doyle will kill you—he's killed men on the outside, I'd stake my stripes on that. Hell, he threatened to kill Lieutenant Redington, and look what—" He stopped.

"You mean Doyle killed that lieutenant?" I said.

"Forget you heard that. I don't know who killed him.

Just keep away from Doyle. And what's so special about that locket of yours, anyway, that you're willing to risk your life over it?"

"It's personal," I said.

Morgan sighed. "You're going to be a hard case about this, aren't you?"

"If I have to be."

Back at the barracks, I checked out the weapons. Peaches and a few other men sat on their footlockers, watching as I sighted down the carbine barrel.

"Don't see why the army got rid of the old Spencer," I said, as I fiddled with the breach-loading mechanism. "I'll take seven shots over one, any day."

"You have used the Spencer?" asked the moon-faced young German, whose name was Hans Kleg.

"Carried one at the end of the war. Took it off a Yank."

"The Springfield's better for long range firing," Dick went on. His first name was Richard, and that, plus his good looks, had led to the inevitable nickname, after the dime novel hero. "That's what they tell us, anyway. We only fire 'em twice a year, to see if they still work."

"The ammunition, it costs too much to do more," Peaches explained.

"Long range firing is fine," I said, "if your enemy stays at long range. Might be better to have a repeater if he's attacking you, especially if you're outnumbered."

"That'll never happen out here," grunted the old soldier, who was called Whitey. "I been chasin' Injuns since before the war with Mexico. They never stand and fight. They always run away."

"Indians have a way of surprising you," I said.

Dick Daring laughed. "Any Injun wants to surprise

me, he better do it before next September 11, 'cause that's when my ass gets discharged."

There was time before mess call, so I took a look-see around the post. I ended up on the west side, behind Officers Row. It was mid-morning, the sky low and gray and threatening, a bitter wind blowing down from Canada. To either side of me were wooden blockhouses, the last bastions of civilization. Beyond them, the bleak prairie stretched to the horizon and beyond, into the unknown. Somewhere out there the Sioux and Cheyenne, under Sitting Bull, were said to be preparing a last stand against the white tide, a fighting farewell to their free lives.

I had problems of my own. On one hand I had a young officer, murdered for no apparent reason. On the other hand, the officer's men didn't want to talk about his death. Were they hiding Doyle, and, if so, why? He didn't seem the type to inspire sympathy. Or were they, as Calhoun had suggested, simply following the soldier's code — don't betray a fellow enlisted man.

And what about that red-haired reporter, Miss Winslow? How did she fit into this? She must have been the one Calhoun was talking about when he said they were having a hard time hushing up the affair. What made her think that Redington's death was from other than natural causes?

I couldn't just go and ask her. When you join the army you give up most of the everyday freedoms you take for granted, among them the one where you can go and talk to people when you feel like it. If I left the post now, I'd be absent without leave, liable for arrest and a stint in the guard house.

"Hughes!" a harsh voice interrupted my thoughts.

I turned and saw Sergeant Varden approaching, bouncing on the balls of his feet. "Captain Keogh needs somebody to clean his latrine. You just volunteered. Get a shovel and wheelbarrow from the company shed — Corporal Wild will show you — and report to Officers Row."

I got the shovel and a barrow filled with dirt and quicklime, and I wheeled it to Officers Row. The latrines were assigned according to rank, grouped from west to east in descending order, as were the officers' quarters. Lieutenants shared one latrine, captains another, majors and lieutenant colonels a third. The post commander had one to himself. At the far eastern end was a large privy for the servants. Myles Keogh waited by the captains' latrine, tapping his leg impatiently with a swagger stick. When I was within a few feet, I put down the barrow, came to attention, and saluted.

Keogh returned the salute, touching his rakishly tilted forage cap bill with the swagger stick, whose silver tip was shaped like a dog's head. I didn't know much about him then. I later learned that he had been awarded two medals by Pope Pius IX for his service in the Papal Guard against the Piedmontese. Following that, he'd come to America and fought in the last two years of our civil war. He'd been with the Seventh since its inception in 1867. Right now, I could have sworn he was tight, as well.

"I thought Varden would send you," he said. There was just a hint of his native Ireland in his voice. "Bloody waste of time if he hadn't. What happened to your face?"

"Somebody's fist fell into it."

"Better get to work."

The latrine consisted of a zinc-lined box. When the box was full, it would have to be taken out, emptied, and the material inside burned. Right now, the mess just needed to be covered with a layer of dirt and quicklime, to cut the stench. I removed the stained seat, which was tricky since the floorboards were badly warped, and a misstep could send me plunging through one of the gaping holes into the box.

"You Irish, Hughes?" said Keogh. We were alone here, so he could be informal.

"Texan," I replied. He gave me a sharp glare, and I added, "Welsh, by descent."

"Welsh, eh? Sing a lot?"

"Not a note."

His jaw clenched. I think he wanted to upbraid me for not calling him "sir," but was held back by the realization that I wasn't really a soldier. He leaned against the latrine wall while I began shoveling dirt into the box. "The General said I should speak with you. To be honest, I don't see why we need a detective. Be easier to beat the truth about Redington's death out of these brutes. A bloody shame the army's got rid of flogging—it's a grand spur to a man's memory." From his greatcoat, he took a piece of paper. "Here's the list you asked for."

I stopped what I was doing, looked around to be sure we weren't being watched, and unfolded it. It was the names of the twenty-five men who'd pulled guard detail the night Lieutenant Redington was murdered. The five men from I Company were underlined. One named leaped out at me—Doyle.

"Thanks," I said. "Tell me, what do you know about Bucko Doyle?"

Keogh grinned—he must have heard about my fight with Doyle from Varden. "Is Doyle really a suspect, or is this just because you don't like him?"

"I don't let personal feelings interfere with my work, Captain. Doyle warned me off the subject when I started asking questions about Lieutenant Redington. Did he have problems with Redington?"

"Doyle has problems with anyone in authority." Then Keogh remembered something. "There was an incident, about two weeks ago. Peter — Redington, that is — went to the post traders', where he encountered Doyle drinking beer. Doyle was supposed to be on duty, so Redington told him to return to the company. Doyle said he'd go, but not till he'd finished his beer, as he'd paid for it. Redington ordered him to leave immediately. Doyle said he'd be damned if he'd leave his beer for a shavetail lieutenant. Redington called the guard. He had Doyle punished and fined two weeks' pay."

"What kind of punishment?"

"He was bucked and gagged."

"Is that when Doyle threatened to kill him?"

Keogh's dark eyes opened wide. "Doyle threatened him? I hadn't heard that."

"Sergeant Morgan told me."

Keogh pressed the silver-tipped cane to his lips. "Doyle. Yes, I can see Doyle as the killer. Doyle was on guard that day, he could easily have slipped away from the guard house, or his post. All you need now is proof, and you can be on your way. Personally, I thought the killer was Tarr."

"Tarr — is he an older fellow the men call Whitey?"

"That's him. Amos Tarr, thirty-year man. Been a soldier since I was five. He was a sergeant till Redington busted him to the ranks last month."

"What for?"

"Tarr had a working party out. I can't remember what

they were doing—whitewashing rocks, possibly. Peter Redington came by, and Tarr didn't salute quickly enough for his taste. To make it worse, Tarr took the salute for his men instead of making them stop work and salute, too. So Redington busted him."

"And you let him get away with that?"

"I had no choice. The system wouldn't work, otherwise. Countermand a junior's orders once, and there's no stopping it. You end up with anarchy—and the army's no place for anarchy."

"I thought Lieutenant Redington was popular with the men. He seems to have been a real donkey's ass."

Keogh bristled. "This is the Regular Army, Hughes. It takes discipline, and lots of it, to keep these men in line. Redington didn't do anything I haven't done myself."

Then why did they kill him and not you, I thought.

From the guard posts, the sentries called out the hour followed by, "All's well." On the parade ground, a bugler sounded "Recall From Drill." "Hurry up and finish with that sink," Keogh said, pulling a cigar from his coat. "The stench is killing me."

I got back to work. "What can you tell me about Redington's personal life?"

Keogh lit the cigar, turning his back to the wind. "Not much. He didn't like being posted to the Seventh—not at first, anyway. He wanted to be back east—a staff post in Washington or New York. He hoped to marry a wealthy woman, and he didn't think he'd find one out here."

"He needed money?"

"Need might be too strong a word, but he certainly wanted money. 'Genteel but impoverished' is how we describe his type in Ireland—God knows, Ireland's got enough of them. That's what Mrs. Custer told me, at any rate. The regiment was in the field when Redington got here, in July. When we returned, in September, he seemed quite happy with us. The bracing frontier life changed his mind, I suppose—and, of course, the prospect of learning his soldier's trade under General Custer."

"Financial problems notwithstanding?"

"He didn't seem to worry about them anymore."

"And his body was found . . ?"

"About two hundred yards west of Guard Post Three—that's the beat between the first two blockhouses. And if you think it's strange the guard saw nothing, it's because he was probably hiding in one of the blockhouses, to get out of the wind."

"You knew?

"Of course. They all do it. We're not going to be attacked by Indians this time of year, what's the point in having the guards freeze to death?"

"How big was Redington?"

Keogh was clearly ready for this interview to end. Probably he needed another drink. "Look here, Hughes, we seem to have established that Bucko Doyle is the killer. What difference—?"

"I'm trying to figure out if one man could have carried the body, or if there had to have been more."

Keogh let out his breath. "Peter was smaller than me—about five-seven, I guess. Maybe a hundred and sixty pounds."

"So one man—a strong man like Doyle—could have carried him that far, but it would have been difficult. Lieutenant Calhoun told me Redington had been beaten. How, exactly?"

"His skull was fractured. By the proverbial blunt instrument."

"A pistol barrel?"

"That's my guess. But he died from the cold. If you'd seen him, you'd know that. Stiff as a board, poor bastard, though he didn't turn blue, the way they say it happens in books. Maybe he hadn't been dead long enough, I don't know."

"Any other marks?"

"There were bruises on his face and body."

"So he'd been assaulted with fists, as well?"

Keogh hesitated. "Apparently."

"I understand he was in his underwear. Were his clothes found?"

"They were next to the body."

"Was anything missing—anything of value?"

"His watch. It was the only expensive thing he owned—a silver Hamilton, with his name engraved inside the case."

"So—find the watch, find the killer. Why the hell didn't you tell me that in the first place?"

Keogh's black eyes blazed, and he lashed my shoulder with his cane. "Watch your mouth."

The force of the blow drove me backwards. I lost my balance, and one of my feet broke through the rickety floorboards into the latrine pit's ooze.

I rose and pulled my foot free, shaking off the muck. I could feel it squishing around inside my shoe. I turned to Keogh. "Touch me with that cane again, and I'll stick your head in this hole."

Keogh grinned hugely, enjoying my predicament, the cigar propped in one corner of his mouth. "Try it, and I'll see you spend the rest of your life in Leavenworth."

"You think that'll stop me?"

Keogh dropped the grin. His eyes met mine. He

hefted the cane, as if deciding whether or not to use it, then let it fall to his side. Stiffly, he said, "As to the watch, I didn't mention it because whoever took it is bound to have gotten rid of it by now. Sold it in town—thrown it away. Even a Welshman would realize that watch is evidence enough to get him hanged."

It was all I could do not to pop the bastard. "It would be risky to sell the watch in town," I pointed out, "at least right away. A valuable piece like that attracts attention in the hands of privates. And I can't imagine a common soldier throwing it away, not when it represents potential income to a man making thirteen dollars a month. I'd hang on to it and wait for the dust to settle. There's always places to hide it. I knew one of Mackenzie's troopers who hid whiskey bottles in the guardhouse walls. Got himself assigned to the construction detail and stashed the bottles in hollowed-out adobe bricks. That way when he—"

"This is the Seventh Cavalry," Keogh interrupted, "an elite unit. Colonel Mackenzie's regiment hardly bears comparison. Now—if you're quite done with me?"

"For the moment," I said. "You've been no end of help."

Keogh pulled out his orderly book, scribbled something on a page, tore it out, and gave it to me. "The General wants to meet you. Finish what you're doing here, then get cleaned up, and report to his house right away. If anyone asks your business, you're taking this message to him."

CHAPTER 8

The first flakes of snow swirled around me as I approached General Custer's house. I mounted the steps to Custer's wide veranda and banged on the door. It was opened by a moon-faced black girl. "Message for the General," I told her, showing her Keogh's scribbled paper.

She held out her hand. "I gives it to him."

"I was told to deliver it personally."

"General Custer, he be working. I see he gets dis message."

"Captain Keogh told me to—"

"What is it, Mary?" chimed a bell-like voice.

"Sojer with a message fo' de Gen'ral, ma'am."

There was a rustle of skirts, and a slight but commanding woman appeared. "I'll see to it," she told the maid, who nodded and went back to work.

I doffed my forage cap. "Private Hughes—Lysander Hughes—to see the General, ma'am."

"Come in," said the woman, shutting the door behind me. "I'm Mrs. Custer."

"My pleasure, Mrs. Custer."

Elizabeth Bacon Custer might have been attractive in her youth, but approaching middle age had turned her mousy and prematurely gray, with thin, disapproving lips. She looked me up and down, frowning at my scar. "James Hickok says you're reliable and discreet, Mr. Hughes. I trust that you are—especially discreet."

I noticed that she used Hickok's given name,

45

something only his best friends did. Rumor had it that Libby Custer had gone ga-ga over Hickok in Kansas—she wouldn't have been the first woman to fall for him—but her affections had not been returned. That wasn't surprising—Bill's tastes ran to whores and half-breeds.

"What else did Wild Bill say about me?" I asked her.

"He said that you were the best-read man he'd ever met."

Knowing the type of men Bill hung around with, that wasn't much of an endorsement. "Kind of him to say so."

"Have you read my husband's book, *My Life on the Plains*?"

"No, unfortunately. I've read several of his articles in *Turf* and *Galaxy*, though. They're very well written."

"The General is waiting for you down the hall, in his library." Libby touched my sleeve. "Peter Redington was such a well-liked boy. He had a good future ahead of him -- my husband had taken him under his wing, you know. Why anyone would kill him, I can't imagine. I do hope you'll get to the bottom of this."

"I'll try, ma'am."

"Deeds like this blacken the regiment's name. My husband will get the blame for it, too, you'll see, when it's none of his fault—just like they blame him for everything." She sighed. "His life has been very hard. He's had to overcome any number of obstacles to get where he is. Even now, there are men—some of them in this very regiment—who conspire against him, for no other reason than jealousy over his great success."

"Yes, ma'am."

I made a half bow to her and went down the hall. As I did, Libby returned to the large parlor, where I heard the laughter of men and women—officers and their wives.

Glancing through the open door, I saw that they were playing blind man's bluff. Weren't these men supposed to be on duty?

Unlike the other quarters on Officers Row, the post commander's house was huge; it even contained a ballroom with a chandelier. The Custers' furnishings were sparse, however, befitting the nomadic army life — mismatched and battered chairs, tables fashioned from boxes, rugs made from old blankets edged with calico. Indian artifacts adorned the walls. The library door was ajar; I rapped on it and went in.

At first glance the room looked like an attic, cluttered with stuffed animal heads and military bric-a-brac. Against a wall was a moth-eaten couch with one leg propped on books. As I entered, there was an explosion of movement from the couch, and a large stag hound leaped off it, followed by the man who had been using the dog for a pillow. The man sprang to his feet, casting off a Mexican blanket which he wore round his shoulders against the cold.

I stopped in astonishment. I had expected to see the famous Boy General with his flowing locks, but Custer's hair was cut short. Not only that, he was going bald. He was thirty-six, but could have passed for fifty. His cheeks were hollow and sunken, like a consumptive's, highlighting prominent cheekbones which were set off even more by his shaggy moustache. There was not an ounce of fat on his lean body, though, and his pale blue eyes burned with a keen intensity I have seen in few other men.

"General Custer?" I said as the dog sniffed my shoe. "I'm Lysander Hughes."

"Our detective, eh? Forgive me for not being

prepared for you, Mr. Hughes. I was taking a catnap. Don't mind Blucher there, he's harmless." He took a swat at the dog. "Get away, Blucher." The dog came right back, still sniffing, and Custer said, "He must like that smell. What happened to you, anyway — fall in Keogh's latrine?"

"Something like that."

Custer laughed. He wore a blue vest over a white shirt, and uniform trousers. The room smelled of the cinnamon oil he used on his thinning hair. One look at him made it obvious why he'd let the hair grow long originally — to hide as prominent a set of jug ears as you'd ever want to see. He indicated the desk. "Been putting the finishing touches on my latest article for *Turf, Field and Farm.* Enjoyable work, writing, but darned hard on the eyes. It goes to the publishers after Christmas, so I've a lot of work to do. Everyone tells me I should write my wartime memoirs. Can't think why I haven't, really — Heaven knows, plenty of lesser men have. Maybe it's because there's so much to tell. It would take longer to write than it did to fight the war."

He laughed at his joke. My eyes were suddenly attracted by movement on his head. I looked more closely. "Excuse me, General, but there's a mouse in your hair."

Custer reached up. The mouse, as though trained, ran onto his finger. Custer brought it down, stroked it. "This is Diodorus. I found him in this room, raised him. I didn't think he should be deprived of his freedom, so I set him loose in the field, but he came back. He likes me, you see. Animals always do."

He put the mouse on his desk, and it scurried into an empty inkwell, which had been turned on its side and filled with bits of paper and straw. Near the inkwell was a framed portrait of Libby in her wedding dress. On the wall above that were photographs of Custer and General Sheridan. On the other walls had been mounted stuffed antelope and deer heads. More hunting trophies were scattered around the room on pedestals—a sand hill crane, mountain eagle, great white owl and several species of fox. There was a gun case in one corner. From antlers and animal heads hung hats, sabers, spurs, map case and field glasses. But the room's centerpiece was a stuffed buffalo head above the mantel.

"Excellent specimen, eh?" said Custer, indicating the buffalo. "Brought that back from the Black Hills two years ago, for Libby. Thought she'd put it in the sitting room, but the dear insisted it go in here. I shot the creature myself. I'm the best shot in the regiment—the best shot in the army for all I know. Stuffed it myself, too—the buffalo head, that is. I stuffed an elk out there, as well, but it was too big for the house, so I shipped it to the Detroit Audubon Museum. Ever tried taxidermy, Hughes?"

"Can't say that I have."

"Interesting hobby. Relaxing after a day in the field. I'd like to do a bear next. Put it in the front hallway to frighten tenderfeet from the east—especially government bureaucrats." He laughed again. "Tom says we should stuff Sitting Bull when we catch him, but I think that's a bit extreme. Libby would never allow it anyway."

Custer rubbed his long fingers together, warming them, while he looked out the window. "Snowing, I see. We'll have a foot on the ground by morning." He turned back to me. "I'll be honest with you, Hughes. I'd have preferred a man from the Pinkertons, but Libby insisted we hire you, on Bill Hickok's say so. You ask me, a recommendation from Hickok is like saying you believe in little green men, but my wife will have her way. Tom almost had apoplexy when he heard about it."

The dog Blucher had climbed back onto the couch and lay with his head hanging down, his eyes following his master's every movement. From the parlor came a burst of laughter. Custer said, "How long have you been a detective?"

"I've been working for myself about six years now."

"And before that?"

"I was on the San Francisco police force."

"You quit to go into business for yourself?"

"No. I got kicked off."

"Why?"

"Trouble with my captain. He was corrupt, I wasn't. He won. I became a detective sort of by accident. Right after I left the police, a fellow hired me to find his missing wife."

"And did you? Find her, I mean."

"Yes, though things didn't work out the way everyone expected. Anyway, when you're successful at a job once, word gets around. People keep hiring you. Pretty soon it's what you do for a living."

Custer had begun pacing back and forth. The room couldn't contain his boundless energy. The fort couldn't contain him—I doubt the entire prairie could have contained him. He was like a caged tiger—no, with his lean, hollow-cheeked looks, more like a wolf. "Cooke tells me you're from Texas. I was in Texas after the war, part of the military occupation force." He paused. "I suppose you fought in the war?"

"Yes."

"You in any of my battles?"

"Never got that far east. Only fight I was in that you

might have heard of was Palmito Hill." I'd also taken a reluctant part in Quantrill's raid on Lawrence, Kansas, but I thought it best not to mention that.

"Palmito Hill, I know about that. An embarrassment to our arms." Jocularly, Custer added, "It would have been different had I been in command, of course. I am reminded of Napoleon's dictum: 'In war it is not men that matter. It is the man.' "

I should have kept my mouth shut, but I'd had enough of this insufferable ass. "I doubt that, General."

He stopped pacing. His keen eyes fixed mine. "What?"

"Against Rip Ford and those men? On our own ground? You wouldn't have stood a chance, not unless you had a division with you, and if that was the case, you'd never have brought us to battle."

Custer's visage, which until now had been sunny, clouded. His corded jaw muscles worked. "I beg to differ with you," he said icily. "I never met a Rebel general I couldn't beat. I beat Jeb Stuart, I beat Mosby. I would have beaten Forrest—or Bobby Lee himself, if you come down to it. So I doubt I would have encountered any difficulty with your Doctor Ford. Now, let us get to the reason you're here. Have you learned who killed Lieutenant Redington?"

"I have a suspect. No proof yet."

"I'm making an important trip back east after the first of the year, and I need this wrapped up before I go."

"That doesn't give me much time."

"No. My brother Tom and Myles Keogh think you can just flog the truth out of these men. I'm sure you can, but can you imagine the outcry if we did that and Congress got wind of it? I've gotten in trouble before for trying to instill real discipline in this regiment. I have enemies who would demand my head this time—they came close to getting it last time. We've kept Lieutenant Redington's murder out of the papers so far, but it wouldn't take much to blow the lid off. My enemies would have a field day. When the truth about this incident comes about, we want to present it as a *fait accompli.*"

"That the only reason you want the case solved?"

"I don't follow you."

"You don't seem too concerned about finding the killer for Lieutenant Redington's sake."

"Of course I am. He was a fine young officer. A tragedy what happened to him. How dare you suggest I don't care about him?"

"Just an impression I got."

"By Geoffrey, let's get one thing straight, Hughes. I don't tolerate impertinence."

"No, General, you get one thing straight. I'm not one of your troopers, I'm just the hired help. If I don't like what's going on here, I can always give back your front money and walk."

A slow smile formed under Custer's walrus moustache. "That's where you're wrong."

"What do you mean?"

"You signed enlistment papers for five years. If you don't find Lieutenant Redington's killer, I'll see that you serve every day of those five years."

"You wouldn't do that."

"Wouldn't I?"

"You can't do it. Before I left Cheyenne, I had Lieutenant Calhoun draw up a paper specifying the terms of our agreement—in case something happened to you. I had it witnessed and left it with a prominent lawyer. If I can't get out of my enlistment, he'll take it to a judge."

"Let him," said Custer. "I'll deny everything. It'll be your word against mine, and who is a court going to believe—a man who was kicked out of the San Francisco Police, or me?" He smiled wickedly.

"What about Calhoun?" I said. "And Cooke? And Myles Keogh?"

"They do what I tell 'em."

"What about your wife, then? She knows who I am."

"If you think Libby is going to get you out of this, you don't know Libby. She's the last who would tell, believe me. And if you try to run away, I'll have you tracked down and shot as a deserter." His smile widened. "So you see, Texas, you have no choice but to find the killer."

I said nothing. I wanted to beat the bastard to death with his buffalo head, but they'd shoot me for sure if I did that.

"Is there anything you need before you go?" Custer asked.

It was hard to think, I was so mad. "Who were Redington's best friends?"

Custer tugged his moustache. "Odd question. I suppose he was closest to Lieutenants Erickson and Granville. Granville's the man Redington replaced in I Troop. He's Quartermaster now, attached to A. Anything else?"

"I'll let you know," I said. He stiffened expectantly, like he was waiting for me to salute, but I was damned if I'd salute him in private like this. I turned to the door.

"One thing puzzles me, Hughes."

I stopped.

"What were you doing in San Francisco? Why did

you leave Texas?"

"I killed four men."

Custer turned up his nose. "Saloon brawls, I suppose?"

"Not at all. I shot them in cold blood. Good day, General."

CHAPTER 9

I left Custer's house and returned to the task of finding Lieutenant Redington's killer. My meeting with Custer had been a disappointment. I'd come to Fort Lincoln expecting, if not to like Custer, at least to admire him. After all, he'd been a major general at twenty-three; if nothing else, he must have a good deal of military ability. But a few minutes alone with him had changed all that. I'd never met a man so consumed by his own self-importance. I was surprised he didn't have mirrors rigged around the fort so he could watch himself as he rode by — he probably would have, if he could have figured out a way to do it. As for his military abilities, I didn't know about them yet, but I did know one thing — he wasn't going to keep me in the army for the next five years.

For the moment, though, I was a professional soldier, and I returned to that task, as well. Life in the Regular Army centered around the ceremonies of guard mount and evening parade. Most of our training was to prepare us, not for war, but for these two routines, and even that training was pretty much catch as catch can, because there were a lot of details and fatigues to pull, and you caught one nearly every day. The most important detail was water hauling — there were no wells at Fort Lincoln, so all of the post's water had to be brought up from the river. When the river froze, as it was doing now, ice had to be chopped, then melted down. There were also supply, firewood, and hay distribution details. There were kitchen detail and latrine detail; as well as police details for the company area, parade ground, Officers Row, and stables. There was barracks cleaning and barracks orderly. There were also details for construction around the fort, for painting, and for logging. Skilled men like Peaches, who had carpenter's experience, could earn twenty cents a day at some of this extra-duty work; the rest of us were just forced labor.

On Saturday night, Sergeant Varden gave the company passes into town. The regiment hadn't been paid in months, so most of the men had no money, but no one cared. We just wanted to get away from Fort Stinkin', as the men called it. I had some of Custer's hundred dollars tucked away for an emergency, but I was supposed to be a penniless ex-rancher, so I left the money hidden. No matter—I had other reasons for wanting to go into town.

Dick Daring was our savior. He reported his overcoat as lost (which it wasn't) and drew a new one against his clothing allowance. "I should get at least twenty dollars for this new coat in Bismarck," he said, as he shook it out and showed it to us in the barracks. "That's enough to get us all drunk. I might even be able to get my pole greased if I can find a real cheap whore."

Dick was getting out next September, so it was unlikely he'd need a new overcoat before then. "Get yourself an old coat to wear in the field, Pretty Boy," he told me as we got dressed (Doyle's nickname for me had stuck). "Buy one at auction when somebody gets out or dies. Clothes get ruined in the field, and if you turn out for guard or parade in a ratty coat they'll gig you."

I thanked him for the advice, and we set off for town. There was our group of four plus Hans Kleg, the young

German. Kleg was one of the new men, and he preferred hanging around with us, as his own group was a pretty rough lot. Custer had been wrong about the snow. Instead of a foot, we had gotten two, with a few more inches the following day. We thought nothing about the three-mile slog through the white stuff, however. Most of the company was going, moving in little knots along the road to the steam ferry in the rapidly fading December light.

"River's just about froze solid," Two-Bit observed as we waited to make the short ferry trip. "Be able to walk across in a few days."

"Good," said Dick Daring. He turned to me, explaining. "We lose three or four men each year, drown or get swept away trying to swim the river to Bismarck after 'Lights Out.' "

Once across the river, we went to the Point, a devil's den of saloons and whorehouses directly opposite the fort. Heavy wagons had churned Bismarck's snowy streets into a calf-deep porridge of mud, excrement and urine. It took an enormous amount of supplies to keep Fort Lincoln going, and there were a lot of teamsters in town. There were off duty soldiers, as well, along with cowboys, farmers, and miners staying in Bismarck for the winter before heading for the Black Hills. The saloons had started putting up Christmas decorations. Music played; men were laughing and singing.

As it turned out, Dick got twenty-four dollars for the coat. Whiskey was more expensive if you got it by the drink, so to stretch our money, Dick bought a bottle of rye, and we stood on a street corner in the frigid air, passing it around. "God damn," Peaches giggled as he swallowed the fiery liquid. "Cock suck." Two-Bit Henderson howled at the moon, and Hans looked unsteady on his feet—he couldn't hold his liquor well. When it was my turn, I touched the bottle to my lips but didn't drink. I liked to be clear headed when I was working.

When the first bottle was done, Dick tossed it into the street. "Let's go down to the Bull's Head and see the hoochie-koochie dancers. Then we'll get another bottle."

As we started off, I dropped back and separated myself from the others. I'd tell them later that I lost them in the crowd. I went around the saloons, asking bartenders and customers if they knew where I could get a cheap watch. Several people had watches to sell, but none were silver Hamiltons with Peter Redington's name engraved on them. I still believed that Redington's killer had kept the watch to unload at a later date, but I had to be thorough.

I spent several hours at this. My head throbbed from the stifling heat of the saloons, from the pounding, off-key piano music, the blue clouds of tobacco smoke. My scratchy woolen underwear was plastered to my body by sweat, which turned to ice every time I went back outside.

I stopped to relieve myself behind the Black Kat. As I did, I heard a muffled cry further down the alley. It was a woman's voice. Likely some fool had taken a whore back there, instead of going inside where it was warm. There was the cry again—this time it contained a note of distress, and I heard people struggling. Whatever was going on, it was none of my business.

I went down the alley to investigate.

Ahead I saw shadowy figures in the snow. A man's accented voice growled, " . . . or the next time we cut your throat. You *comprenez* that?"

There was a muffled squeal.

A second man said, "What do you think, Louie—let's do 'er."

The woman was struggling harder now, trying to scream through whatever they had over her mouth.

"Non," said the man with the accent. "You 'ave heard the boss—"

"Nobody'll know. She's a prime piece, and I'm horny as a stud bull. She won't tell nobody. She'll be too embarrassed."

There was a pause, then the man with the accent said, "Very well. You hold her, and—"

"What's going on here?" I said.

The figures separated—two men and a woman, one of the men noticeably taller than the other.

"Let's go," said the shorter one, the one with the accent. In the reflected light from the snow I saw a beard with a white streak down the middle. His tall companion swore with frustration, then the two of them ran down the alley. I would have figured them to fight, but maybe they thought I had more men with me.

The woman leaned against the building, shaken. I put a hand on her shoulder. "You all right?"

She recoiled from my touch. "Get away!"

"Easy," I told her, "I'm on your side." Whores were always being beaten or raped. This one probably figured I came to finish what the other two started. Then I peered at her more closely. I had seen her before. "Miss Winslow!"

Her green eyes came alert, recovering from the shock. Blood dripped from a thin cut on her throat. "How do you know my name?"

"I saw you in the Adjutant's office the other day. What are you doing in this part of town?"

"You may have saved my life, but I don't see where it's any of your business why I'm here."

"It's got something to do with Lieutenant Redington's death, doesn't it?"

She straightened her tall form, suspicious now. "Why do you say that?"

"Just a guess. I heard you say you're working on a story about it."

"You seem to hear an awful lot."

"Lieutenant Redington was my company officer. I liked him. I want to see his killer brought to justice."

"So he *was* murdered," she said, and a small smile of triumph creased her lips.

"Yes, but no one's supposed to know that. How did you find out?"

"I have an informant."

"At the fort?"

She pulled a handkerchief out of her coat and dabbed the blood from her throat. "That's right. I was supposed to meet him here tonight. But those men attacked me first. They put a knife to my throat—that's how I got this cut. They warned me to stop asking questions about Mr. Redington's death. They said, if I didn't—well, you heard them."

We left the alley, emerging onto the crowded street. "Who is this informant of yours?" I asked.

She laughed. "Nothing doing, Mister—?"

"Hughes. Lysander Hughes."

"Well, then, Private Hughes. First, you tell me what you know about Mr. Redington's death."

I shrugged. "Just that the killer is a soldier, like me."

"That's not what I heard."

"What do you mean?"

"My informant says Redington was killed by another officer."

"Are you serious?"

"Dead serious—if you'll pardon the play on words."

"What officer?"

"That, my informant hasn't told me. Yet. You seem unusually curious for a soldier, if that's what you really are."

"What do you mean? What else could I be?"

"I'm not sure, but I'll let you know when I figure it out. In the meantime, perhaps you could help me with this story. I'd be willing to pay for information."

Part of my job was to see that the story didn't get in the papers, but I was curious to learn how much this Winslow woman knew—and how she knew it. "All right," I agreed. "What do—"

"Verity!" cried a man's voice. "Verity, there you are!" A young officer came rushing toward us, nimbly hurdling the frozen ruts of the street. "What are you doing here—what can you have been thinking of?" He saw the cut on her throat. Then he saw me. "Son of a—"

I was on my back in the mud before I realized that he'd hit me. Before I could react or say anything, he leaped on me, snarling, grabbing my overcoat with one hand while his heavy fist thudded into my face again and again.

"Reed—stop!" yelled Verity. "Reed—leave him alone!"

She grabbed the officer's arm with both her own and stopped him in mid-swing. With a struggle, she pulled him off me. "It wasn't him that did this. He saved me from them."

The officer moved back reluctantly, crimson with

rage. He looked like he still wanted to hit me.

I lay in the mud, collecting my wits. While I waited for my eyeballs to stop spinning, I ran my tongue around my mouth to see if any teeth were missing.

Verity moved closer to me. "Are you all right?"

"Not really," I said. I could feel my face swelling. The bruises had just started to go away from the last beating I'd gotten.

The officer pulled me to my feet. I shook my head, blinking, and my feet shuffled around with a will of their own till I recovered my balance. The officer, a first lieutenant, said, "Sorry about the misunderstanding, soldier."

"I'm not too thrilled about it myself."

His eyes narrowed. "Speak properly when you talk to an officer. Who are you?"

"Hughes—sir. I Company."

"I Company, eh? My old outfit. You must be a new man, I don't recognize you."

I saw a surprised look cross Verity's face. I'd told her I'd known Redington, implying I'd been with the company for a while. "This is Captain Reed Granville," she told me. "Captain during the war, that is—he's a lieutenant now."

"Officers don't introduce themselves to enlisted men, my dear," Granville corrected her gently.

Verity told Granville how the two men had jumped her and how I'd run them off. She didn't mention the Redington story. Likely this Granville was following the official line with her about that, and she didn't want him knowing that she was still working on it.

"What were you doing at the Point?" he asked her.

"Checking out a story for Mr. Lounsberry."

"Why didn't you tell me, so I could come with you?"

"You're at the fort. I can't come and get you every time I have to work."

"Tell somebody else, then—that fellow Kellogg, for instance. You shouldn't be in this district by yourself, it's too dangerous." To me he said, "Hughes, it seems we owe you a debt of gratitude." He put one arm around Verity's shoulder, while he took her hand in his. "I certainly do, anyway. Sorry again about the misunderstanding."

"Yes, sir. Thank you, sir."

He smiled down at Verity. After a second, he looked back at me. "You may leave, Hughes."

"Yes, sir," I said, saluting. "Glad to be of help, sir."

I watched Granville lead Verity Winslow away. She looked back over her shoulder at me once. Then they were lost in the crowd.

Verity said Granville had been a captain during the war. He couldn't be more than twenty-seven or twenty-eight now; he must have been a kid, then. I remembered Custer saying that Granville had been one of Redington's close friends. He also hit hard.

I thought about the two men who had attacked Verity. The last time I had seen the short one with the streaked beard, he'd been sitting in the office of Haselmere, the post trader; and I was willing to bet that his tall companion had been the man with the red bandanna on his head that day. Was Haselmere the "boss" who had ordered them not to hurt Verity Winslow?

It was time to pay the post trader a visit.

CHAPTER 10

I returned to the fort, but not to the company area. The post trader's establishment stood by itself, off the northeast corner of the parade ground. The guards paid the store regular visits — its valuable merchandise and its liquor supply made it a tempting target for thieves. I was out of bounds here, and I kept to the shadows as much as I could, which was difficult because of the snowy background. It was freezing cold. The prairie wind sang through the eaves of the buildings. Overhead, the stars burned with crystalline brilliance in the December sky.

The store proper, the bar and pool room, and the warehouse were in one building; the stables and wagon shed in another; and the trader's house beyond them. No lights burned in any of the buildings. It was well past midnight; Haselmere must be in bed.

I stole onto the store's veranda. No guards about. No sound save the keening wind. I picked the door's two locks and slipped in. Reflected light from the snow outside brightened the room, which smelled of sawdust and the licorice candy Haselmere kept for the kids. Before I did anything else, I went into the bar room and stuffed my overcoat pocket with whiskey bottles. I opened one of the bottles and rolled some of the fiery rotgut around my mouth, to taint my breath. I spit it out, then poured about half the bottle's contents into a spittoon before putting the bottle in my coat with the others. Then I went into Haselmere's office, which was where I had seen the two teamsters who jumped Verity Winslow.

I pulled down the window blind, struck a match and lit the kerosene lamp. The light might give me away, but it was a chance I had to take. The small office was neatly kept, its chief feature a massive safe in one corner. I'd come back to that safe later if I had time. There was a stack of papers on Haselmere's desk. I took them and sat on the drafty floor, between the desk and the wall. I found a blanket and pulled it over myself and the lamp, to further screen the light.

What I had was a block of invoices from the Sioux City Cattle Company, covering several months' worth of the beef that Haselmere purchased for the post. He bought all the beef from this same supplier, in lots of from ten to two dozen head—one to two weeks' supply— paying from fourteen to thirty-one dollars a head, depending on the season, reselling it to the fort for two dollars a head more. There were also invoices for flour, which Haselmere purchased in large amounts from a consortium called Missouri Valley Grains, as he did most of the other goods he sold.

None of this established a link between Haselmere and Lieutenant Redington, though. What kind of link would they have had—could they have had? Redington had only been in Dakota a few months before he was killed. Maybe the two teamsters had accosted Verity Winslow under the auspices, not of Haselmere, but of the officer who had supposedly murdered Redington. Maybe the whole thing was a put on, somebody pulling Verity's leg, making a fool of the intrepid girl reporter—in which case I was exposing myself to a lot of needless risk by being here. Because to me, Bucko Doyle still looked like the murderer. Sergeant Morgan thought Doyle had done it. So did a lot of the men in the company; I could sense it by the way they acted around him.

Footsteps outside.

I turned down the lamp's wick and threw off the blanket. It must be the guard, walking his post. The footsteps crunched loudly in the crusted snow, then mounted the veranda. The guard stamped his feet, trying to warm them. I heard him blowing on his hands. If he turned and noticed that the locks were open, I was dead. Seconds passed. The man stamped his feet some more and kept going, footsteps receding in the snow.

I waited a minute, left Haselmere's office and entered the warehouse through the connecting door. There were no windows in the warehouse, and I re-lit the lantern. There were scrabbling noises, blurs on the floor, as mice scurried from sight. The musty building was jammed with barrels and boxes of all sorts of goods—food, blankets, bolts of cloth, rifles, pistols. There wasn't enough money at a frontier fort to support this kind of operation. Haselmere must make most of his profit from the civilian trade.

Sliding double doors led onto the loading platform, barred from inside. I tried them; they were locked. I wouldn't have opened them in any event, it would have made too much noise. My shoe snagged on something on the floor. Some kind of sacking, partly jammed under one of the doors, probably missed after clean up. With difficulty, I worked it free and held it to the lantern. It was an empty, 100-pound grain sack. On it was stenciled "U.S. Indian Agency."

I stared at the sack for a moment, then let it fall back to the floor. Time to go. I'd learned all I could for one night. The office safe would have to come later. Blowing out the lantern, I opened the connecting door and stepped into the darkened store—to find myself facing two soldiers with leveled carbines.

"Hold it right there," said the sergeant of the guard, looming behind them. "Get your hands up."

I did as he commanded. The sergeant took the lantern, re-lit it, then set it on the counter. As the shadows resolved themselves, I saw Haselmere in the background, smug satisfaction on his face. He wore a coat with an expensive astrakhan collar; a Smith & Wesson .45 was in his hand. "I told you there was someone in here, Sergeant," he said. "I was on my way home from town, and I was certain I saw a light moving inside the store."

"Don't know how the guard missed it, sir," the sergeant apologized. He was a tall drink of water with a shaggy moustache.

Haselmere took the oversight with grace. "These things happen."

To me, the sergeant said, "I don't recognize you, Scarface—who are you?"

"Hughes. I Company."

"What are you doing in here, Hughes?"

"Nothing, Sarge."

"Nothing? Nothing, is it? What's in them coat pockets, then? Search 'im, Windham."

While one guard covered me with his carbine, the other pulled the whiskey bottles from my bulging coat pockets. He held the half-empty bottle up for the sergeant to see. "Here's what he come for, Sarge."

The sergeant smelled my breath and recoiled. "Helpin' yerself to Mr. Haselmere's goods, were ye, ye drunken sod?"

I shrugged helplessly.

Haselmere stepped closer, and a smile of recognition split his oily face. "Why—I believe it's my old friend Lysander with an 'L.' It seems you're the robber, this time, Lysander."

"You were doing such a good job at it, I thought I'd have a go myself," I told him.

"Save yer jokes for the mill," the sergeant said. "March 'im off, lads."

CHAPTER 11

"I knew you was no good, Hughes," said Sergeant Varden. "I could tell from the moment I first laid eyes on your sorry ass."

We were in the company office, a glorified shed behind the barracks. Company punishment was rated for my crime. Captain Keogh and Lieutenant Porter were there, as well, sitting in chairs behind Varden's desk. Varden recited the charges, his pugnacious eyes boring into mine. "'Intoxicated on post, breaking into the trader's store.' By rights, that little adventure should get you a month in the mill, plus stoppage of pay. But I'm going to be generous, Hughes, since Christmas is almost here. You'll be bucked and gagged for the remainder of the day and fined two week's pay." He turned. "Agreed, Cap'n?"

Keogh nodded, a twinkle in his eye. He was enjoying this, the Black Irish bastard. Lieutenant Porter gave him a questioning look, but Keogh didn't acknowledge it.

I said, "Permission to speak to the Captain, First Sergeant. In private."

"Denied," said Varden casually. To Sergeant Morgan, who stood behind me, Varden said, "Take him behind the barracks and carry out the sentence." Keogh made no attempt to intervene, to hear what I had to say. He was more interested in demonstrating his authority over me than in finding a brother officer's killer.

Morgan marched me off, guarded by Blorm and O'Connor, two men from my platoon. "Why'd you do this, Hughes?" Morgan said. "I didn't take you for the type."

"Don't rightly know, Sarge. Whiskey got hold of me, I guess. I barely remember any of it."

"You'll get a chance to sober up now, that's for sure. Sergeant Varden's from the old school. Believes in physical punishment."

"You don't?"

"Never seen that it does any good. Makes a lot of men worse, from what I can tell."

They took me behind the company area. The land here sloped down to the river, affording a good view of Bismarck and the endless prairie beyond. Blorm and O'Connor, who was nicknamed Malaria, cleared a spot free of snow.

"Sit down," Morgan ordered. "Hands round your knees."

I complied. Morgan tied my wrists and ankles with rawhide thongs. He placed a stick beneath my knees and across the crook of my elbows, pinioning my arms in place, then stuck a filthy bandanna in my mouth. The bandanna tasted awful, like it had been in a hundred mouths before mine. They must have kept it for just this purpose. Morgan tied the bandanna behind my head, then checked to make sure all was secure. "Wish I could take it easier on you, Hughes, but Varden would have me out here if I did. Good luck."

He turned. "Detail—atten-tion! About—face! Right shoulder—arms! Forward—march!"

He led them off, counting cadence. I sat alone in the snow. Morgan had left me exposed to the wind. There were no sheltered spots, but he might at least have turned my back to it. I guess he was worried about getting in trouble with Varden. He was too close to getting out to lose his stripes now.

The sun had been out earlier, but now the sky was gray. The wind blew out of the northwest, at the left side of my face. The position they'd placed me in put an extreme amount of stress on the shoulders and back, but the pain in my back was the last thing on my mind right now. The cold was first. It sliced through me like that Comanche war axe had gone through my face. I'd been cold before, plenty of times, but nothing like this. I couldn't move. I couldn't do anything to get the blood circulating. It wasn't long before my teeth were chattering like Spanish castanets. Shivering was my body's only defense, and soon I was jerking back and forth spasmodically, as if I were having a seizure.

I lost track of time, caught in my agony of cold. Stables must have been over because a couple men from A Company wandered by. "Who's that?" said the first one.

"Some new fellow," replied his companion. "Heard he got nailed stealing booze from Haselmere's store."

"Dumb ass. Least he could have done it without getting caught."

They were replaced by a different group. "What's this?" crowed Bucko Doyle. "Why, it's Pretty Boy Blue."

"Blue's the right word for it," said his companion, Malaria O'Connor. "Lookit his face."

"Stupid fuck'll do anything to get off fatigue," added another man named Smith, who was called Alias.

"Lookit that dance he's doing," Malaria said. "Better'n them girls at the Bull's Head," opined Alias.

I tried to curse them through my gag, but my jaw muscles were frozen tight.

"What's wrong, Pretty Boy?" said Doyle. "Not so tough now, are you?" He made a snowball and thwocked me in the face with it, just below the eye. It snapped my head to one side; the icy snow stung my skin.

The other two laughed. They made snowballs, as well, winding up and hurling them like baseballs, as hard as they could—and at that distance it was just about impossible to miss. The morning's sun had partially melted the top layer of snow, turning it to a half-frozen slush just right for snowballs. I had no defense but to lower my head and endure, as the frozen missiles blasted my face and chest. They knocked off my cap; they rocked my skull.

"All right, Doyle, cut it out." It was Dick Daring.

There was a brief scuffling and cursing above me, then Doyle and his pals left, laughing among themselves.

Dick and my friends bent close. I had a hard time seeing them through my swollen face and the tears in my eyes. The splattered snowballs were turning to ice on my cheeks, and Dick wiped them off. "Hang in there, Pretty Boy. You'll make it."

"Jeez, Pretty Boy," said Peaches. "You don' look so good."

"They must let you go soon," said Hans Kleg.

"They better," Two-Bit Henderson added ominously.

My friends stayed a few minutes more, encouraging me and trying to make me comfortable, though there was little they could do. Then the mess triangle sounded and they went to dinner, leaving me alone in the gathering gloom.

Time passed. I stopped shivering. I no longer felt cold. My body had gone numb. I wanted to close my eyes and sleep, but I knew what the consequences of that would be. My remaining energy was concentrated on staying awake. I wondered if Lieutenant Redington's last thoughts had been much like my own right now. Was it coincidence that I was out here bucked and gagged, just as he had been, or was there more behind it?

Across the river, the lights were winking on, injecting a bit of cheer into the gloom. I wondered if those lights were the last thing I would ever see. My eyelids closed in spite of myself. I lifted them again, but they were, oh, so heavy. They kept closing, closing . . . closing . . . .

"Untie him," said a voice from deep inside my dream.

The stick was pulled from beneath my knees. I was hauled to my feet, my hands and ankles freed. Gloved hands were slapping my face to bring me around.

"Give him some of this," said the voice.

Something metallic was tilted to my lips. I swallowed. Brandy. It jolted warmth into my stomach, brought my eyes swimming into focus. I saw Peaches and Hans Kleg; behind them, Lieutenant Porter. Hans and Peaches held me up. I couldn't stand — my legs were numb from the cold and prolonged sitting. I made an effort at moving my limbs, getting blood into them.

"You're free to go," said Lieutenant Porter. He was a fair-haired young man with a strikingly intelligent face. Gentleman Jim we called him, because of his well-bred air and good manners.

"Thank you, sir," I mumbled through numb, swollen lips.

"Thank your friends here," Porter said. "They came to my quarters and got me. They were afraid you would freeze to death."

Maybe that had been the plan, I thought.

"I don't know what Sergeant Varden was thinking of,

putting you out here in this weather. The Captain said he would set you free, but I guess he forgot about you for one reason or other. Now, get back to the barracks and get your gear in order. Second Squad's been alerted for ten days in the field. We leave at first light."

CHAPTER 12

It was late afternoon. Second Squad, I Company, was camped on the Heart River, some fifty miles west of Fort Lincoln. There were twelve enlisted men, two non-coms, Lieutenant Porter, and a civilian teamster in charge of the pack animals. We huddled around fires in our groups of four, drinking coffee and fixing supper. There were several feet of snow on the ground, and the temperature felt like it was a hundred below zero, though it was probably only minus ten or twenty. The bluffs behind us afforded some protection, but the wind still set our tents snapping.

We were on a ten-day scout to investigate reports of Indians leaving the reservations to join Sitting Bull's "hostiles" — the government's term for Indians who wanted to live free. If we found any, we were to intercept them and return them. If they wouldn't go, we were to kill them. We had started at the Standing Rock Reservation, where Schofield, the Indian agent, had appraised Lieutenant Porter on the situation. From the reservation we had followed the river. Several times we had come upon tracks heading west, at least till they were buried by a fresh snowstorm, but we had been unable to catch the men who made them.

Mess responsibilities in my group of four had been laid down long before I joined. Peaches and I built the fire. Dick Daring made the coffee, roasting the green beans in a skillet, then smashing them with his revolver butt and covering them with boiling water. Two-Bit Henderson prepared the food. Right now he was cooking what he called skillygalley. First he boiled off our day's ration of salt pork, then fried it. He soaked our ancient hardtack, crumbled it with the ever-useful revolver butt and added it to the pork, stirring it in the grease. It was so cold we couldn't even smell the food cooking. We held the tin coffee mugs under our noses to let the hot fumes unfreeze our nostrils.

"What are you going to do when you get out of the army?" asked Dick Daring.

Peaches answered Dick's question first. "Me, I going to get the good job. I work with my hands—" he held them up, though they were covered with heavy buffalo skin gauntlets just now—"I work with wood. I get a woman, build house. Raise big family."

Two-Bit was next. "Wa-a-ll," he said—he could make a word last all day with that Midwestern twang. "I got me a hankerin' to see some more of the country 'fore I go home. Think I'll go on down to Arizona when I'm done soldierin', maybe Mexico—always wanted to see Mexico. Might even get to your neck of the woods, Pretty Boy—Texas. Most likely I'll end up in California. Seems like everybody ends up in California."

"You ain't going home?" said Dick, sniffling against the cold. "Thought you had a girl back in Indiana."

"Naw. Went off with some other feller. I'll get back home one day, I reckon. Just ain't in no hurry."

Hans Kleg sat in the snow by our fire. Behind him, Bucko Doyle and the rest of Hans's group were roasting their salt pork on wooden spits. Hans said, "When I get out, I stay right here."

"Here by this fire?" asked Two-Bit.

"No," said the moon-faced young German. "Here in Dakota. I will get free land. I will farm. The land, it is very good."

"The land, it is very cold," said Dick. "Too much winter for me."

Dick had scrounged a box of raisins from somewhere. Now Two-Bit added them to his pork and hardtack mixture, stirring them in the grease to plump them. Sergeant Morgan wandered by and warmed his hands over our fire. "What are you boys confabbing about?" He handed Dick his cup. "How 'bout some coffee, Daring? You make the best coffee in the regiment, if I do say so."

"We're making up stories about what we're going to do when we get out of the army," Dick said. He filled Morgan's cup from our pot and handed it back. "What about you, Sarge? You're getting married, ain't you?"

Ice hung from the tips of Morgan's moustache, making it droop even more than usual. "That's right. Going back to Ohio. Gonna buy me a nice farm and settle down."

"You're gonna buy a farm off what you saved from your army pay?" asked Two-Bit skeptically. Sergeants only made three dollars more a month than we did.

Morgan hesitated. "Didn't say it was going to be a big farm," he joked.

Two-Bit stirred some brown sugar into our supper, let it cook through, and pronounced the dish finished. We spooned the concoction onto our tin mess plates. It tasted surprisingly good, and we shoveled it down — awkwardly, because we wore every article of clothing we owned. Besides my overcoat and jacket, I had on two shirts, two pairs of drawers and three pairs of socks. On top of that, we had stuffed every inch of free space in our boots and clothes with crumpled back issues of the Bismarck *Tribune* that the company saved for just this purpose. When we walked, we waddled around like blue penguins, but no one cared how he looked. Gloves were not official cavalry issue, so we wore the clumsy buffalo skin gauntlets sewn by the enlisted men's wives and post laundresses. Some of the veterans had knit wool caps, like sailors wear; others had good quality felt hats they'd bought in town, with wool scarves to protect their ears. The newcomers, like me, wore the regulation black campaign hat, which was made from flimsy wool felt and did little to warm our heads, and our ears were covered by cotton bandannas. All of us had smeared our faces with pork grease as protection against frostbite.

Dick wiped his mouth on the back of his field overcoat. "I think I'm going back to school. Might even go to college. Study law, maybe."

"Go on, get out," said Sergeant Morgan, drinking the coffee.

"I'm serious. I hate the army, but I'll admit it's straightened me out. I ran with a bad crowd back in New York. I was a lot like Bucko, then—a tough yegg, always in scrapes with the law. Most of my pals ended up dead or in jail, and I realized that I was going the same way if I didn't change. So I enlisted. Anyway, if I go to law school, I'll be able to defend all you dead beats when you get in trouble."

"I'd rather you opened a saloon in Bismarck and gave us free drinks," said Two-Bit.

"What about you, Pretty Boy?" said Dick. "Any plans?"

I looked down at my meal. I felt guilty. I was with these men but not of them. I was an impostor. I was under no illusions, either. These men might be my friends now, but they would turn on me if they found out what I really was. They would kill me. "Hell," I joked, "I ain't been *in* long enough to figure out what I'm going to do when I get out."

Sergeant Morgan worked his watch from the depths of his overcoat. "Your turn for guard, Hughes. Relieve Tarr."

In the dying light, I took my place on guard, on the upstream side of the camp, opposite the horse lines. My beat ran along the riverbank, parallel to the brush-covered bluffs at a fifty-yard distance from camp, then back again. I cradled my carbine in the crook of one elbow, with my hands stuffed deep in my overcoat pockets, grateful for the exercise, which helped to warm me. I had a second bandanna that I pulled over my nose to protect my face from the wind. When we'd first left Lincoln, the bitter wind had made my cheek bones ache, like they were being crushed by an invisible force, but I didn't notice that as much anymore.

As I walked, I thought about the patrol's earlier visit to the Standing Rock Reservation. Schofield, the Indian Agent, was an irascible fellow with a sulfurous red beard that stuck out in all directions, like someone had glued a porcupine to the bottom of his face. He reminded me of General Sherman, only with more hair. He had told Porter that none of his Indians were leaving the reservation, and to prove it he had showed him the latest distribution rolls, with nearly all of his charges listed as drawing rations. He didn't know where the rumors were coming from — frightened settlers, he supposed, or people eager to stir up trouble.

It was the first time I had been on one of the northern reservations, where the government was trying to turn nomadic buffalo hunters into farmers. I saw hollow eyed, emaciated women, children with protruding stomachs, old men who would not survive the winter, all of them begging us for food. Some of us handed out our moldy salt pork and weevil-ridden hardtack, which were consumed on the spot. It left us less to eat, but that didn't matter. Others in the squad regarded the scene with sullen indifference.

"Notice anything?" I asked my friends as we waited by our horses for the Lieutenant to come back.

"Young men," said Dick Daring. "There ain't any. Think the stories about them running are true?"

"Looks like. If I was stuck here, I'd be running, too."

Tinker Stafford, one of the October recruits, disagreed. "Why should they run away? Lazy bastards got it made here. They ain't got to work, and Uncle Sam feeds and houses them. Look at them tipis—if they ain't brand new, I'm Abe Lincoln."

"They're made from canvas," I told him. "Indians make their lodges from buffalo hides. The cured skin keeps them warm, and it keeps out the rain and snow. Those—" I waved at the cones of cheap calico print— "won't keep out a thing. The Indians that don't starve will freeze to death or die from disease. This is slow extermination."

"What's wrong with that?" growled Bucko Doyle from down the line, where he was eyeing some of the young women. "It's no more'n they deserve."

A number of the men agreed. "If you'd seen your friends carved to pieces by these red bastards, you'd say the same," said Corporal Wild.

I probably had more reason to hate Indians than any other man here, but I couldn't bear to see this. It would be more humane to kill them outright.

From our visit to Standing Rock, my thoughts ran to that empty grain sack marked "Indian Agency" that I'd found at Haselmere's warehouse.

Then footsteps intruded.

It was dark now, and a tall figure loomed against the snowy background. I pulled my hands from my pockets and came to present arms. "Evening, sir."

"Evening, Hughes," said Lieutenant Porter. He was muffled in an overcoat, scarf and a rabbit-skin cap with thick earflaps. "Everything quiet?"

"Yes, sir." I relaxed. In the field we were more informal than on post, and the better officers, like Porter, would often converse with men on guard.

Porter stood beside me, staring at the star-lit sky. We made small talk about the weather and how we'd rather be in the desert, chasing Apaches. Somewhere a coyote howled. Then Porter said, "Have you had any luck finding Peter Redington's killer?"

I swung round and stared. "Sir?" I stammered, as if I had no idea what he was talking about.

"It's all right. I know who you are."

"You do? How?"

"Myles Keogh was talking about it at the Officers Club. He was in his cups, said he had a recruit who was really a detective looking for Peter Redington's killer. You're the only new man we've had since October."

"Christ."

"That's why I was surprised when he had you tied up. I guess he didn't want to be seen playing favorites — people might get suspicious."

I doubted that was Keogh's real reason. I think Porter doubted it, too. "What's to be suspicious about?" I said. "Half the Seventh Cavalry must know who I am by now. I'm surprised it hasn't been in the Bismarck *Tribune.*"

"He only mentioned it the Club. I doubt it got back to the men in the company."

I was in so much shock from what Keogh had done, that for a moment I didn't even feel the cold. At last I said, "Since you know who I am, could I ask you a favor? I'm supposed to work through Captain Keogh, but . . . "

"I understand. Myles has a rather busy 'social' schedule. What do you need?"

"Two teamsters I saw at Haselmere's store. I wonder if you know them. One's short and stocky, with a white streak in his beard."

"Rene St. Jacques — yes, I know him."

"He has a partner, or he did when I saw him. Tall fellow, kind of ugly . . . "

"Whitehead," said Porter. "I don't know his first name."

"I wonder if you could find out where they were the night Redington was killed. If they were in Bismarck."

"What do they have to do with this?"

"I'm not sure yet. It's more of a hunch."

"You think they killed Redington?"

"I don't know. I do think he was killed by more than one man. The work of carrying the body and undressing it suggests that. Plus the fact that he was so badly beaten leads me to believe he was jumped by — "

"He wasn't beaten by the killer," Porter said. "He got

those bruises in a fight at the Officers Club. Didn't Myles Keogh tell you that?"

Once again I was stunned. "It seems Captain Keogh didn't tell me much of anything. Who was he in the fight with?"

"Lieutenant Manley of the infantry. They busted up the place pretty good. I was O.D. that night, and I had to break it up. Threatened them both with arrest. It was me that made Redington leave the Club. Hadn't been for that, the poor fellow might still be alive."

"What did they fight about?"

Porter seemed to hesitate just the slightest bit before answering. "Nothing important. They were both drunk."

"You probably knew Redington as well as anyone. How did you get along with him?"

"Actually, we didn't see that much of each other. He was acting quartermaster for two months, while Reed Granville was away on court martial duty. We shared quarters, but we didn't have the same interests. Peter liked gambling and drinking. He seemed to be a good officer on a technical level, but he didn't have much skill with men—or interest in them, for that matter. He was too harsh on them, too caught up in himself."

"General Custer liked him, I understand?"

"Yes. Peter admired the General."

"Keogh told me that Redington didn't want to be posted to the Seventh, but was later glad he had been."

"General Jack has that effect on some men."

"'General Jack?'"

"Custer. His initials—G.A.C.—spell 'Jack.' It's the nickname Libby likes us to use."

"The men have another name for him."

"So do some of the officers."

Porter chatted a few minutes more, promised to check on St. Jacques and Whitehead for me, then left. A guard tour was two hours, the time being kept on Sergeant Morgan's watch, which one of the guards carried while Morgan slept. The half-moon rose, providing some light. I paced my rounds in quiet, with the snores of sleeping men, the low crackle of the fires, the occasional stamp or blow from long-suffering the horses my only company. The crystalline cold was so intense, it seemed the rocks would crack. Toward the end of our shifts, Turkey Leddison, the other guard, and I built up the fires. Then we woke our replacements, mine being Hans Kleg.

I walked with Hans a while. I wasn't particularly sleepy, and I wanted to talk to him. He told me about his village in Bavaria, surrounded by mountains. It had been his dream to come to the United States since he was a child. The word "freedom" was a powerful lure for him. In Bavaria his future was foretold. "My father, he was . . . he own store, yes? I would own store, in turn. My son after me. In America, it is . . . different. There is not limit. Here, I can be anything if I work hard."

Eventually I steered the conversation to Lieutenant Redington's death. "Men killing their officer — that ain't usual, is it?" I said as we walked along, heads down against the wind.

Hans shook his head. "In Germany — in Prussia — they shoot entire company for such a thing. Here . . . nothing. Perhaps here is too much freedom sometimes, yes?"

"Maybe. But, come on, you all know who killed him, don't you?"

"No, we do not know. Maybe we think so, but we do not say for sure."

"Well, it's none of my business, but it's pretty clear to

me that Bucko Doyle did it."

Hans's face clouded. "Bucko. I hate the Bucko. He beats shit from me when I come here."

"Did he kill Redington?"

"I did not see it."

"He threatened him, though?"

"I did not—"

From nearby there was a flash and the nearly simultaneous crack of a rifle shot. Hans and I dropped to the ground.

"Indians!" shouted Tinker Stafford, the other guard. He began firing his carbine in the direction of the bluffs, from where the shot had come.

There was shouting and confusion as the rest of the squad tumbled from their tents and started shooting blindly into the night.

"Cease firing!" shouted Sergeant Morgan as he ran up, his overcoat already buttoned. "Wait till you have a target!"

"Form a skirmish line!" bellowed Corporal Wild.

Lieutenant Porter appeared, coatless, pistol in hand. A sudden silence descended on the camp as the men stopped firing and arranged themselves in order. There was a metallic clicking as they reloaded their weapons. "What happened, Sergeant?" Porter asked.

"One shot, sir," Morgan answered. He pointed toward the land at the base of the bluffs. "From over there. Sniper's my guess. Some young buck out to make a name for himself. Hit and run. He's gone now, we'll never catch him."

I rose to my feet, brushing off the snow. "Hey, Hans, it's over—get up."

But Hans didn't get up. He lay on his face, arms

spread. Beneath his head, a dark stain was spreading on the snow.

"Oh, no," I said.

I knelt. One arm flopped across Hans's chest as I rolled him over. Just above his right eye was a large hole—jagged, because the bullet had been tumbling when it exited. Blood and brain matter oozed from the wound, running into his sightless eyes and down his face into the snow.

"Oh, Christ," said Lieutenant Porter with a breaking voice, and I realized he had probably never seen a man killed in action before. Then he made a visible effort and composed himself. He was the officer in command. "Sergeant, prepare the body. We'll take him back to the fort. Double the guard for the rest of the night, in case whoever did this comes back. Dismiss the rest of the squad."

"Yes sir," said Morgan.

Dick Daring came up beside me as I stared down at Hans's body. "Hell of a way for you to get an overcoat," he muttered.

As I started back to my tent, I noticed Whitey Tarr glaring at me. The hate in his eyes produced a cold tightness in my guts, like they were being twisted around. Then somebody grabbed my arm. It was Morgan.

"I thought I told you to settle your problems with Doyle," he said through clenched jaws.

"What are you talking about?"

"You know what I'm talking about. That was no Injun that shot Kleg. I know it, and I think you do, too."

I said nothing.

"That's what I thought," Morgan said. "That bullet came from a .45-70 Springfield carbine, an army rifle. I've heard 'em shot off enough to know what one sounds like. That bullet was meant for you."

Still I said nothing.

"There's no way to prove it was Doyle," Morgan went on. There was a catch in his voice, and I could swear he was fighting back tears. "I could check his rifle to see if it's been fired, but just about every weapon in the squad was fired just now. That son of a bitch killed a good man. A real good man. Never hurt a soul. I'm warning you for your own good, Hughes—keep away from Doyle. And watch your back."

"I will."

Morgan left me alone in the bone-numbing cold.

Somebody—probably Doyle—was trying to kill me. But had he tried to kill me because he hated me, or because he knew who I really was? Whichever, I had better get him before he got me. But there was another force driving me, now. I had liked Hans Kleg. I wanted the man who killed him to pay for it.

CHAPTER 13

Around me in the darkened platoon bay, the men had settled into sleep. The only illumination came from the soft glow of the stove at the bay's far end. It was the first Saturday night since we'd returned to the fort. "Lights Out" had sounded at nine-thirty, about a half-hour earlier.

Quietly, I swung myself from my bunk. I paused to see if anyone was watching, then bundled some clothes under my blankets, hoping the lumpy form would pass for me at the eleven o'clock bed check. Suddenly I stopped.

I wasn't the only one sneaking out of the barracks. Down the bay a hulking form moved among the shadows, easing toward the door.

It was Bucko Doyle.

I let him leave, then dressed and followed. He slipped around the rear of the barracks. I dropped from the veranda and started after him.

It wasn't hard to keep him in view—by now the post streets were little more than tunnels through the ever-accumulating snow. Evening parades had been canceled along with most drill, as Fort Lincoln settled into battle with its most implacable enemy—winter.

There was no one else out. The air was bitterly cold. Doyle headed for the northern end of the fort. He passed the stables and entered the warren of shanties belonging to the married enlisted men and laundresses. He stopped by one of the rude houses, opened the door without knocking, and went in. I heard a snatch of feminine laughter.

At least somebody was having fun tonight, I thought. There was no sense sticking around—I had other things to do. I was scared—being shot at has that effect on me—and I wanted to finish this case while I was still in one piece.

On the way back to the fort, I'd asked Peaches if Doyle had been in the guard house when Lieutenant Redington was killed. "No," Peaches said. "I see him sneak out."

"The sergeant didn't know?"

"Sergeant Vickory, he was asleep. Drunk, I think. Bucko comes back before the new shift."

Allowing time for the sergeant to get to sleep and Doyle to return, that still gave Doyle an hour and a half to kill Redington—plenty of time. But where did he do it? It wasn't in Redington's quarters—there'd been no sign of a struggle there—so he must have caught Redington on the way back from the Officers Club. A hell of a coincidence, to know when he was going to leave.

Unless Doyle was going somewhere else, met Redington on the way, and killed him on the spur of the moment. Which would have been perfect except for one thing—the Officers Club was on the other side of the post from both the guard house and Suds Row.

Unless Doyle was supposed to meet Redington, but why would he do that?

I left the fort, slipping past the guard posts, and started down the road to the Bismarck ferry. As I slogged through the churned up snow, I had the sensation of being followed. Several times I stopped to check my back trail, but I saw no one. I must be getting jittery.

The river was frozen now, and I walked across. In contrast to the quiet of the fort, Bismarck was in full swing—lights, music, crowds, occasional pistol shots as drunks tried to bring down the moon. Christmas was just over a week away; there were wreaths and crude decorations everywhere. I wasn't the only soldier in town, either. There were plenty of men willing to run the guards in order to sample Bismarck's pleasures.

I figured it would be easy to find Verity Winslow. In a town where nine of ten inhabitants was a man, an unmarried woman like her should stand out. I tried the *Tribune* office, but it was closed. I searched the restaurants, but didn't see her there, nor was she in any of the shops still open. I came to McKenzie's Theater and Variety Palace, from inside of which came snatches of dark, dramatic music. The play was *Orlando*—not one of my favorites, but after you've seen the two Bills (Cody and Hickok) in *Scouts of the Plains*, anything seems like a classic. After talking to the fellow in the ticket box, I hung around till the show was over and the crowd poured into the muddy street.

I saw the red hair first, piled in a bun under a fur-trimmed hood. Verity left the theater on the arm of an army officer—Lieutenant Granville. They made a handsome couple, laughing, at ease in one another's company. I followed them. Granville took her to a restaurant, where they had a late meal and made small talk, gazing in each other's eyes, now and then touching hands across the table. Afterwards, Granville walked her back to a boarding house on the east side of town. They went inside. He stayed a bit, then reemerged, mounted his horse, and trotted off through the snow.

I stepped from behind the trees where I had been hiding. Most of the boarding house was dark — the occupants must be respectable citizens who went to bed early. Then a light came on in one of the back rooms. I made a snowball and tossed it at the window. It hit the pane with a soft "plop."

Nothing happened. I made another snowball and threw it. I was patting a third, when the curtains parted and the window rattled open. Verity peered out and saw me. "Who are you?" she said in a loud whisper. "Get away from here before I — "

I motioned her to keep her voice down. "It's Lysander Hughes."

She peered more closely. "From the other night? The soldier with the scar?"

"That's right."

"See here, Private Hughes. You may have done me a favor, but that doesn't give you the right to --"

"I need to talk to you."

"What could you possibly have to talk to me about?"

"Peter Redington."

She hesitated. "Wait there," she said at last. "I'll be right down."

I was stamping my feet in the snow, trying to warm them, when the house's back door opened and Verity came out, muffled in a heavy coat. She closed the door gently, so it wouldn't make any noise, jamming it part way open with the stop. I started up onto the porch, but she waved me to stay where I was and joined me, her breath frosting the air.

"Tell me what you want and be quick about it," she said, shivering. "Mrs. Crosbie, my landlady, doesn't like me having visitors, not even Reed. She doesn't trust single women. She knows I work for the paper, but she still thinks I'm some kind of adventuress. She's looking for an excuse to throw me out."

"I need your help," I said.

"What kind of help?"

"Those men who jumped you the other night—the ones that warned you off the Redington story? Their names are St. Jacques and Whitehead. They work for the post trader, Haselmere."

"I know Mr. Haselmere," Verity said. She stuck her hands in her armpits to warm them. "You're not implying that he sent them after me? That's ludicrous."

"Somebody sent them after you. I've learned that Haselmere buys all his beef and most of his supplies from two companies—Sioux City Cattle and Missouri Valley Grains. I need you to check on them and see what you can learn."

"Why? What can that have to do with Lieutenant Redington's—"

"I don't know. That's why I want you to check. I'd do it myself, but I can't get away from the fort."

She looked askance at me. "What are you up to? Are you trying to throw me off the story? Peter Redington's death had nothing to do with Amos Haselmere."

"Then why were Haselmere's men after you?"

She had no answer for that. "Are you sure your only interest is in avenging your officer's death?" she said after a minute.

"I'm sure."

"Why get me to help you?"

"You're the only one I can trust. You're the only one with access to the outside."

"And anything you learn about the murder you'll

share with me?"

I had to tred lightly here. Verity and I were at cross purposes. She wanted a story, a big splash to make her career. Part of my job was to keep the story from the public eye. "That's the deal," I said. "And any information you have, you'll share with me — right?"

"You mean, like the name of my informant?"

"That would be a start."

"I'm not ready to go that far yet, but I'll check on your companies. Lord, I can't stand this cold any longer. Come upstairs a minute while I get a pencil and write down those names. And for Heaven's sake, be quiet."

We went inside. The warmth of the house felt like heaven after the sub-zero cold outside. "Never heard of a woman reporter before," I said as we tiptoed up the back stairs. "How'd you get into this game?"

"What business is it of yours?"

"Just wondering."

"If you must know, my father owns a paper back in Ohio. I grew up in the business. My parents sent me to a fancy college to learn a lot of useless things — manners and how to act superior, mostly. They expected that I'd come home, get married, and turn out grandchildren for them. But I wanted to work on the paper. My father and brother wouldn't let me — they said it was man's work, that I couldn't do it. I was determined to prove them wrong, so I left home and struck out on my own."

We went into Verity's room and she closed the door. The room was small and neatly kept, save for a desk piled with notebooks and pencils, along with pens and an inkwell. The only sign of Verity's occupancy among the sparse furnishings was a small, silver-framed photograph of an older couple whom I took to be her parents.

She went on. "I won't bore you with my adventures; but, suffice it to say, I learned there's precious little work for women out there—certainly nothing in the news business. Finally, Mr. Lounsberry, the *Tribune*'s publisher, took a chance on me. I'm determined to break a big story, to justify his faith in me."

"Striking a blow for women?"

"I'm striking a blow for no one but myself," she said, rubbing the cold from her hands. She picked up a pencil and notebook. "Now, what were those names? Sioux City Cattle was one, wasn't—"

There was the click of a key in the lock, and the door was thrown open.

We both turned to see a small, beady-eyed young woman with her hands on her hips.

"By all that's holy," said the woman, "I knew it! I knew what you was up to, and now I've caught yez. Entertaining sojers at all hours. One coming in the back, and the other barely out the front—and this one not even an officer."

Verity said, "Mrs. Crosbie, it's not what you think. Private—what was your name again?—and I are discussing a matter pertaining to my business."

"Aye, to be sure ye are," the beady-eyed woman sneered. "Discussing how much it'll cost him to get you on your back, I'm thinkin'. Well, I'll have none of yer shenanigans here, ye shameless Jezebel. Pack yer things and get out."

"But, Mrs. Crosbie—"

"This minute!"

CHAPTER 14

That was how I found myself, at midnight, carrying Verity Winslow's considerable luggage through the Bismarck snow, struggling to keep up with the luggage's red-haired owner, who stomped on ahead, a lone hat box in her hand.

"Reed told me to keep away from enlisted men," she said. "I should have listened to him. Because of you, I no longer have a place to stay. I hope you're happy." She stopped and piled the hat box into my already overloaded arms. "Here, take this."

"Now I know how Sancho Panza felt," I muttered.

"How would an enlisted man like you know about Sancho Panza?"

"I read the book."

"You can read? How extraordinary."

"It helps to pass the time when I'm not raping and pillaging."

"And did you learn anything from this book?"

"I learned that Sancho had all the brains, and his partner ran around chasing windmills."

She whirled on me. "Is that what you think I'm doing—chasing windmills? I've a good mind not to help you at all." She started walking faster.

"Fine," I said, following with my burden, slipping in the icy ruts. "Find Redington's killer by yourself, then. Which brings up a question—if this informant of yours knows so much, why hasn't he told you the killer's name?"

"He wants money for it. Two hundred dollars. That's why he approached me in the first place. He told me about the killer being an officer to pique my interest. I don't have that kind of money, though, and Mr. Lounsberry won't commit such a sum without proof."

"Does the fellow have proof?"

"Nothing physical. Only what he saw."

"Did it ever occur to you that this might be a trick? A way of conning money from a gullible reporter?"

She stopped again. "Are you saying I'm gullible because I'm a woman? I suppose you think I should be home changing diapers or looking after a husband?"

"That part's true, but I'm saying you're gullible because your informant's story stinks worse than an upset skunk."

"Sometimes one must take risks, Private Higgins."

"Hughes."

"This man says his life will be worthless if he tells me the murderer's name. He wants the money so he can desert and start a new life."

"I'll bet he does." It sounded like her informant was an enlisted man. That took Lieutenant Granville off the hook, anyway.

I heard light steps in the snow behind us. I turned to see a large yellow dog. The dog stopped and grinned at us.

"Where did he come from?" Verity said.

"I don't know." Maybe the dog had followed me from the fort. Maybe he was the cause of that queer sensation I had felt—was still feeling.

Verity stooped. "Come here, boy. Come here."

Slowly, a few feet at a time, shying away then coming

forward again, the dog approached. Verity let it sniff her hand, then petted it. "Good boy. Good dog." Suddenly the dog started licking her face like she was its long lost mother.

I rolled my eyes. I thought a dog would have had more sense than to throw itself at Verity Winslow. Maybe I felt jealous, as well—after all, it was me the animal had been following all night. Why should it start showering affection on someone else?

Verity rose and began walking again. The dog trotted beside us now, occasionally branching off to sniff at something and pee on it. "Are we going anywhere in particular?" I asked Verity. "Or are you just trying to get me some exercise? These bags feel like they're filled with rocks."

She ignored me.

"Did you ever meet Lieutenant Redington?" I went on.

"Yes, at various social functions. I can't say I cared for him. He was charming, but shallow, like a lot of men. Impressed with himself."

"Did he . . ?"

"Try and get me interested in him? Oh, yes—more than once. He had more hands than an octopus. But, like I said, he wasn't my type. Anyway, I was already seeing Reed."

"Granville? What did he say about it?"

"I don't think he knew. Peter always made his advances when we were dancing or getting refreshments."

"You didn't tell him, then—Granville, I mean?"

"No. Why start trouble when it's not needed?"

"And now you think the story of Redington's death is

going to make your career?"

She tossed me a superior look. "It's just the start. I intend to accompany General Custer and his regiment on their campaign. I intend to write a story that will get the attention of the entire nation. I'm going to write the truth about the army's extermination of the Indians."

"Sounds like you've got the story written already."

"Except for the details."

"What makes you think Custer will let you go with him? He's not big on negative publicity, you know, and accusing one of his officers of murder may not be the best way of ingratiating yourself with him."

"That's the beauty of it—after the Redington story, Custer won't be able to exclude me from the expedition. There would be an uproar. People would accuse him of retribution, and he's too chivalrous to allow that. Besides—the General should be happy with me for solving the crime for him. He doesn't seem to be doing anything about it on his own."

I couldn't agree with her reasoning, but there was no denying that she was determined. "The campaign is supposed to push off in February. That means snow and cold—living in it, never getting warm. If you survive that, you'll have to deal with the heat, the dust, the thirst of summer. All the while, you'll be surrounded by men, with never a moment's privacy. Can you handle that?"

"If the men can do it, so can I."

"You'll probably want to bring all these suitcases, too. I just hope you don't think I'm carrying them. What does Lieutenant Granville think about this?"

A crack showed in her wall of self-confidence. "He doesn't like it. He's like you—he doesn't think girls should be allowed to play with the boys."

"How'd you get hooked up with him, anyway?"

"You ask a lot of questions about matters that don't concern you."

"Part of my charm."

"Rudeness would be a better word for it. If you must know, we met at a Fourth of July picnic sponsored by the Lounsberrys. We got on well together, and one thing led to another. Believe me, I was as surprised as anyone. I never intended to get involved with a soldier."

"He won't like you writing a story calling the Seventh Cavalry a bunch of killers."

"I know, but I have to do my job."

"He might say the same thing."

"Yes, I suppose he might."

"You said he was a captain in the war. He must have been pretty young."

"He was eighteen," she said proudly. "He commanded his own company. He won the Medal of Honor—that's how he was made an officer. He's terribly frustrated by the lack of promotion. He never dreamed he'd still be a lieutenant after all this time."

"For somebody that dislikes the army, you seem impressed by his accomplishments."

"The war was different. It was fought for a just cause. All the young men joined up. Now—except for the officers, of course—the army is a collection of criminals and ne'er-do-wells."

"Thank you. Which category do I fall under?"

"I'm not sure yet. Criminal, probably."

We were in the north end of town, now. There wasn't much traffic. This was where the genteel folk lived. Suddenly Verity said, "Thank heavens. They're awake."

We approached a frame house, whose picket fence

was half submerged in snow drifts. A light shone from the parlor. We climbed onto the porch, and Verity knocked on the door, from which hung a large Christmas wreath. I set down Verity's bags. My shoulders felt so lightened, I thought they might lift off from my body, like helium balloons.

The door opened, revealing a prematurely bald fellow in his early thirties, holding a cigar and wearing a sweater. "Verity!" he said. "What the—?"

"I've lost my room, Mr. Lounsberry. I wondered if I might stay with you and your family until I can find accommodations. I have nowhere else to go."

"Certainly, my girl. Certainly. Come in, come in." He stopped when he saw me. "Who is this?"

"Private Hughes, from the fort. He's helping me with my story."

"Ah." Lounsberry spoke in the manner of a man who didn't understand and who was reluctant to ask questions.

I carried Verity's bags inside. From the parlor another man emerged—dark-haired and serious, about forty, also with a cigar. Behind him I saw a chessboard and a decanter of whiskey—evidently he and Lounsberry had been interrupted in the middle of a game. "Good evening, Verity." The dark-haired fellow brightened, and for a moment I think he believed she had come here to see him.

"Good evening, Mark." To me, she said, "This is Mark Kellogg. Mark writes occasionally for the *Tribune*."

Lounsberry's wife came down the steps, tugging a dressing gown around her ample frame. "What's all the— oh, hello, Verity."

"Verity's been turned out of her quarters," said Lounsberry. "She wants to stay here until she gets settled."

"Of course. I'll fix a bed in the spare room." She had a thought. "You know, C.M., I believe the Pfeiffer cottage on Second Street is vacant. Enoch went back east, said he couldn't stand the winters here anymore. Verity might be able to rent it for a while—there certainly won't be any buyers before spring."

"That would be perfect," Verity said.

Kellogg frowned. "Wouldn't it be dangerous—her living by herself?"

"I've got protection," Verity said, and she turned. "Where did he go?"

"Hey!" shouted Lounsberry, and he ran into the parlor, where the big yellow dog was helping itself from a tin of biscuits near the chessboard. "Get away from there!" He shooed the dog out of the room. The dog grinned, like it was proud of itself.

"Is he yours?" Kellogg asked Verity.

"He seems to think so."

The dog stood on its hind legs, put its muddy paws on Lounsberry's shoulders, and began licking his face. "What do you call him?" Lounsberry asked, shoving the animal down.

"I think I'll call him Sitting Bull," said Verity.

"Looks like he could use something to eat," said Mrs. Lounsberry.

"He looks like he'll eat anything that's not tied down," Kellogg said.

I cleared my throat.

Verity looked at me. "I'll just be a second," she told her hosts, and she followed me out the door.

Outside, I said, "I won't be able to get back into town for a few days. I've got guard duty tomorrow, and I'm detailed as barman for a party at Custer's house the night after. Can you get that information by Tuesday?"

"I'll try," she said.

"Good, I'll meet you — "

There was the snow-muffled thump of hoof beats. Sitting Bull charged onto the porch, hackles up, barking.

Verity and I turned to see Lieutenant Granville ride up. He threw himself from his horse, looped the reins over the rail without looking, and ran onto the porch. "There you are, Verity," he said, taking her arms. "Gosh, I've been worried about you. There was something I'd forgotten to ask you, so I went back to the boarding house, and that awful Crosbie woman told me what she'd — " He saw me, and his eyes widened. "You again. Mrs. Crosbie told me there was a soldier in Verity's room. I didn't believe her. I should have known it was you."

He started forward, but I held up a hand. "We're off duty, Lieutenant. You take a poke at me this time, I'm going to poke back."

Granville began stripping off his overcoat. "That's fine with me, mister."

Verity grabbed his arm. "Please, Reed. He's here because — because I asked him to come. He's helping me with my story. I told him I'd pay him. If he's in trouble, it's my fault."

"Is that true Hughes?"

My eyes met Verity's for the briefest moment. "Yes, sir."

"Verity," said Granville, "how many times must I tell you — there is no story. Peter Redington was not murdered. And you," he said, turning to me, "how dare you take money from this lady? What kind of game are you playing?"

I said nothing.

"I'm going to let you off this time, Hughes, because Verity—because Miss Winslow asked me to. But you are to cease all contact with her—is that understood? You are an enlisted man; Miss Winslow is a lady. You belong to different worlds."

"Yes, sir."

"If I see you with her again, you'll answer to me personally. Now, get back to the post."

I saluted and left, with a wink at Verity. As I left the porch, Verity took Granville's arm. "What was it you forgot to ask me?"

"There's to be a military ball at General Custer's house on Christmas. I wanted to know if you'd come with me."

"Of course, Reed. You know I will."

"Good," he let out his breath with relief, and she led him inside, where he was warmly greeted by the Lounsberrys. Sitting Bull barked once at me, as if to reiterate Granville's warnings, then he followed the couple inside, leaving me by myself in the snow. Well, that was the story of my life.

I wondered if Granville knew who I really was. He didn't act like it, but you could never be sure. Had he been at the Club when Keogh was running his mouth? If not, maybe one of the other officers had told him about it. Did he think I was trying to solve a crime or trying to steal his girl?

I hadn't the slightest intention of obeying Granville's order to stay away from Verity Winslow. I would meet her on Tuesday. But there was a lot of work to be done before then.

CHAPTER 15

Next day, at breakfast, Bucko Doyle knocked a cup of scalding colored water into my lap. The army called it coffee.

I half rose, biting back a yowl of pain.

"Sorry if I burned your balls," Doyle said with his lopsided grin. "It ain't like you was using 'em for anything."

I started after him, then stopped. Sergeant Varden was watching. If I did anything, Varden would dump me in the mill, and that was the last thing I needed right now. I gave Doyle a look and resumed my seat.

"Let it go, Bucko," said Malaria Conner, pulling Doyle away. "You two been circlin' each other like a couple of Kilkenny cats."

"Yeah," said Bigfoot Broadhurst, another of Doyle's pals. "It's over."

"No, it ain't," Doyle told them. "Not till I say it is."

I returned to the barracks, where I put on my Class A uniform and fell in for guard duty. Sunday was the best day to catch guard, because that way you missed the weekly company inspection. At Post Headquarters, Sergeant Major Sharrow formed the guard, then marched us to the guard house, where we would remain for the next twenty-four hours, except when on duty.

My first job was "chasing" prisoners. There had been a fresh fall of snow overnight, and the streets needed shoveling. An Englishman from F Company named

Ruddew and I took a group of prisoners to work on Officers Row. The officers' houses were pretty under the new snow, masking their makeshift construction, making them look like a village in a Currier and Ives print.

As the prisoners shoveled, there was a jingling of bells, and a group of officers, led by General Custer and his brother Tom, drove up to the Row in improvised sleighs made from packing crates. The edges of the crates had been carved and scalloped, then painted, and wagon tongues and runners attached—all this done by army carpenters on company time. There was a merry hallooing and joking as women emerged from the houses, wrapped in layers of blankets and furs. The women bundled into the sleighs where hot bricks were laid at their feet. It was easy to pick out Mrs. Custer, even under the layers of clothes, by the way everyone deferred to her.

A pretty, dark-haired woman came last, hurrying because she was late. She got in a sleigh driven by Lieutenant Van Riley of F Company. As she did, one of our prisoners poked his partner. "Look, Charlie—there's Mrs. Manley. What a piece she is. Wouldn't I like to—"

"Shut yer yap and keep shovelin'," Ruddew told him. "This ain't no social 'our. And keep yer eyes off the orficers' women."

With more laughing and calling, the sleigh party set off, spraying Ruddew and me with snow as they went by. I brushed myself off, as the merrymakers disappeared to the west. "Must be nice to be an officer, and come and go as you please," I mused. "I wonder if they ever get drunk and get in fights, like we do."

"Too bloody true they do, mate," said Ruddew. Ruddew's name had been on the guard list for the night Lieutenant Redington was killed. "They're no different from us, for all they put on airs. Mister Manley and Mister Redington got in a real rouser a few weeks back. Tore piss out of the Orficers Club. I know, 'cause I was part of the detail what 'ad to break it up."

"What were they fighting about?"

He winked at me. "You'd 'ave to ask Mrs. Manley about that."

"Mrs. Manley?" Then it dawned on me. "You mean her and Redington — ?"

"Fornicatin' like bleedin' monkeys, they was. Everybody on post knew it — you can't keep no secrets wiv people all jumbled up like this. That fight was the same night young Mister Redington died."

"Think the two events were connected?"

"Not my business, mate. I could care less about Mister 'Igh-and-Mighty Redington. 'E was one o' them stuff-shirted little shits out of West Point. What I 'eard, though, from a mate 'o mine what works at the Club — was that after we left, Manley, 'e 'ad another drink and went to finish the job."

"Then what happened? Wasn't Manley arrested, or at questioned?"

Ruddew snorted derisively. "Wouldn't expect 'im to be, would jer? You watch, they'll drop the axe on some poor sod of an enlisted man for it, if they charge anybody at all. That's the bleedin' army for you. It's no different from England — the orficers stick together. One of 'em could shoot the bleedin' Queen in full sight of a regiment, and they'd swear it never 'appened that way. They'd say some private done it."

Which was exactly what they were saying.

That thought occupied me the rest of the day and into the night as I relieved the sentry at Post Number Five.

Number Five was the magazine, the most out-of-the-way post on the fort. I hadn't been there long when I saw a familiar figure coming down the shoveled walk.

"Halt!" I challenged. "Who goes there?"

"Lieutenant Porter."

"Advance and be recognized."

He did. I presented arms, and he waved me off. "Been waiting for a chance to catch you alone. Thought you might like this." He handed me a cigar.

"Thanks."

He produced a cigar for himself, as well, then struck a match and lit them both. I took a deep draw, savoring the taste. "Some people might say it's dangerous to be smoking next to the powder magazine," I remarked.

"What's life without a little danger? That's why we're in the army, after all. Long as we don't take these things inside, we should be all right."

I smiled.

Porter went on. "It took a bit of doing, but I got the information on your bullwhackers. I'm afraid it's not what you wanted. St. Jacques and Whitehead—his first name is Silas, by the way—were nowhere near Bismarck when Peter Redington was killed. They were on a run to Standing Rock reservation, delivering Government supplies."

So they couldn't have killed Redington. Then why had they warned Verity off the story? And who was "the Boss?"

"Do they work for the Indian Agency or Haselmere?" I asked.

"They're independent contractors, but they mostly work for the Government in one capacity or other. St. Jacques was with the regiment on the Black Hills campaign last year."

"How does a man like Haselmere become post trader?"

"The appointment comes from the secretary of war, Belknap."

"Haselmere doesn't seem like the type of man who would know the secretary of war. He must have friends."

Porter's tone was bitter. "He has a thousand of them."

I looked puzzled, and he explained. "There's talk that the trader's post at Lincoln and half a dozen others are in the gift of Orvil Grant, the president's brother. Grant's asking price is supposed to be a thousand dollars plus a share of the profits."

I whistled. "Must be a lot of profits."

"The post trader has a monopoly on the sale of goods to military personnel. We aren't allowed to buy things in town even if they're cheaper there. It's an official reprimand if you're caught—and in today's army a reprimand can kill any chance for promotion. "

"But Haselmere's making most of his money from civilians."

Porter nodded. "And Indians. He's not above selling Winchesters to the young bucks—for hunting."

"Hunting you?"

"Let's hope it doesn't come to that."

We puffed our cigars, the tips glowing red against the dark sky and white snow. Across the frozen river we could see the lights of Bismarck.

"Christmas in a few days," Porter sighed. "A long way from home and family. But I guess the Seventh is my home now."

Home. Home was something I carried in my saddlebags, and in the brass locket around my neck. I remembered Christmases with the Morrisons, the folks who'd raised me after my family was wiped out. I remembered Lydia Morrison, and my eyes misted.

I wanted to change the subject. "Mind if I ask about something else?"

"Go ahead."

"Why is a thirty-year man like Whitey Tarr in the Seventh? Why'd he leave his old outfit?"

"I wasn't in the army back then, but as I understand it, when the regiment was formed, experienced men were offered a bonus to transfer in. I guess Tarr wanted the money. That, or he figured he had a better chance of making first sergeant here."

"I don't know. Like you said, a regiment, a company, is a man's home. It's his family. And a man doesn't leave home and family, not after twenty years — not unless he has a good reason."

"Maybe he had trouble with an officer, or wanted a chance to serve under Custer. Maybe he thought he'd see more action with the Seventh. Maybe he just wanted a change of scenery."

"Maybe," I said doubtfully.

"Why do you want to know about Tarr? I thought you had pegged Bucko Doyle as the killer?"

"I still don't have any proof. Sometimes I think this case is cut and dried. Other times, it doesn't add up. There's something — or someone — missing, and I can't put my finger on it. General Custer told me that Redington's best friends were Lieutenants Erickson and Granville."

"I'm not sure you'd call them 'friends' exactly. Erickson wasn't in the field with the rest of us last summer, he was left behind as garrison commander. It was only natural that he and Peter would be thrown together. They played a lot of cards from what I hear. Apparently Erickson took Peter for a lot of money — money that Peter didn't have."

"Redington was in debt to him?"

Porter nodded. "As for Reed Granville, he and Peter really didn't spend much time together till after Peter served that spell as acting QM. I guess the experience gave them something in common."

The conversation died again. Porter stayed on till he had finished his cigar. "Will you be at the Custers' tomorrow night?" I asked him.

"Everyone will. It's Lieutenant Manley's birthday." He started to toss away the cigar butt, then stopped, checked that the butt was out and stuck it in his coat pocket. "Something less for the men to pick up on police call tomorrow. If you think of anything else you need, just ask. I want to see this matter cleared up. It's a festering sore in the regiment, and we have more than our share of those already."

He took his leave. I watched him go, tall and confident against the starry sky. Why hadn't he mentioned Redington's affair with Mrs. Manley? He must know about it — unless Ruddew had been lying, but there was no reason to believe he had been. Had Porter been acting out of decency — or did he have something to hide?

I'd told him I needed proof. Tomorrow I hoped to get it.

CHAPTER 16

It was customary to give a man the morning off following guard duty. While the rest of the company got ready for fatigue, I loafed around the barracks, pretending to read a dime novel, called **Buffalo Bill's Oath**, that Two-Bit had lent me. Two-Bit was a voracious consumer of these tall tales; he spent half his pay on them. The book's cover showed our buckskinned hero with one hand solemnly upraised inside a circle of savages, who wore elaborate paint and feathers never seen west of Broadway.

"Fatigue" call sounded, and the company fell out. There had been three other men from I Company on guard with me. Hiley disappeared I didn't know where, and after a while Vaught and Downing wandered over to Haselmere's store to play billiards. I was alone in the barracks. I'd been waiting for this chance since I'd joined up.

I dropped the book, rose from my footlocker, and stole down the bay to Whitey Tarr's bunk. I searched his things—footlocker, clothes, equipment hanging behind his bunk, the gear on his shelf, his mattress—taking care to return each item exactly as I found it. Beads of sweat formed on my brow and upper lip despite the barracks chill. If I was caught, I'd be labeled a barracks thief, and I knew what soldiers did to them. If I was caught by Redington's killer, something worse might happen.

I found nothing.

Looking over my shoulder to make sure no one was coming, I moved across the bay to Bucko Doyle's bunk and repeated the process. I went through Doyle's clothes, running my fingers along the seams and liner of his overcoat, looking for hidden pockets. I laid out Doyle's mattress and felt it thoroughly, working from one end to the other. In the middle, I stopped. There was something in there, something hard. I unlaced the mattress cover and reached inside, my hand fishing through the straw till I encountered something metallic. I pulled it out.

It was a watch.

A silver Hamilton with an engraved case.

I opened it. Inside was an inscription: "Peter A. Redington. West Point. Class of 1875."

I shut the watch, put it in my jacket pocket. Hurriedly I relaced Doyle's mattress and folded it in regulation style. I stepped back into the aisle, studying Doyle's area, trying to see if anything was out of place.

I heard something. Before I could turn, I was thrown against the wall, and a knife blade jammed against my throat.

CHAPTER 17

"What's your game?" hissed Whitey Tarr.

"I'm partial to stud poker, when I play." It was hard to talk with the knife blade against my throat. "Why, are you up for a few hands?"

Tarr shoved the blade up into the angle of my jaw, forcing my head back. "Don't get funny," he said. His face was so close to mine, I could count the few teeth he had left. His rancid breath blasted my face. "You know what I mean. What are you doing here?"

"I've got the morning off, after guard. What do you think I'm doing?"

"I think you're snooping. You been asking a lot of questions about Lieutenant Redington."

I tried to ease the blade's pressure, but it was no use. And Tarr had positioned himself in a way that I couldn't kick him to get free. "No law against being curious," I rasped.

"I'm thinking maybe you're too curious. I'm thinking you were planted."

"Planted by who?"

"I ain't stupid, Hughes. When an officer gets killed, and a week later a new man joins the company, asking a lot of questions, I can put two and two together. They sent in a detective. You from the Adjutant General's office in Washington?"

"I'm from Texas, you jackass."

Our eyes met for a long second, and I thought I was

going to die right there. Then Tarr eased the blade's pressure. "Ah—I can't be certain. That's the only reason I don't kill you now."

"How would you explain my body if you did?"

"Wouldn't have to. One slice—" he drew his thumb across his throat—"and I'd be out of here before anybody was the wiser. Let somebody else explain it."

He stepped back, sheathing the knife under his jacket. I fingered my neck. There was a spot of blood where the knife blade had broken the skin.

I socked Tarr on the jaw, knocking him over Blorm's bunk. "I'm no detective," I told him.

He got up, rubbing his jaw. "Reckon you're entitled to that one," he said. "Just don't try it again."

"Are you the one that took that shot at me when we were on scout?" I asked. "Was that supposed to be some kind of warning?"

"So you know it wasn't Indians, huh? No, it wasn't me. If I'd shot at you, I wouldn't have missed. And I sure wouldn't have hit poor Dutchy Kleg. And since you're so damn curious, I'll tell you something else—that cocksucker Redington got exactly what he deserved. The army's going to make me retire in a year or so—campaigning in the cold and heat makes you old before your time. I've took wounds, been laid low with disease. Never complained, neither, because the army was my life. I loved it. And now I'm going to lose my sergeant's pension, because of some asshole six months out of the Academy. That little fuck."

"Sounds like a confession," I said.

"You just don't quit, do you, Hughes?"

"Part of my charm."

"Go ahead, make jokes. But I'll tell you right now,

you're playing a mug's game. If you ain't who you say you are, you'd better desert. If you don't, you're a dead man."

"Thanks for the advice. I'll keep it in mind."

"You do that."

Tarr left. As soon as he was gone, I went into my overcoat and got part of my hundred-dollar advance that I'd hidden away for an emergency. I threw some dirty clothes in my duffel bag and headed for Suds Row.

Behind the Row's ramshackle houses, groups of stringy-haired women pounded washboards over tubs of hot soapy water. Their hands were red and raw from their labor, and they gossiped in a variety of accents, mostly Irish. Water slopped out of the wooden tubs, melting the snow around them and turning the ground to mud, so the women stood on duckboard platforms to keep their feet dry.

I was looking for a certain Mrs. Nash, wife of a corporal in A Company. The corporal's name was Dolan, but for some reason his wife had kept the name of her previous husband, a sergeant. She reputedly knew more about what was going on at Fort Lincoln than any other person on the post. She also lived next door to Bucko Doyle's girlfriend.

I was directed to a field behind the houses. There I found a lady with a wicker basket full of women's frilly underthings which she was hanging up to dry.

"Mrs. Nash?" I said.

She turned, drawing a veil across the lower part of her face. She spoke with a hoarse voice. "Yes?"

She was as tall as me, rawboned and angular, with thick black hair and eyebrows, and she smelled of cheap perfume. I was surprised by her appearance, because this ungainly creature was the most popular woman in the regiment, the Seventh Cavalry's "super laundress." She was a Mexican, the midwife at every birth, the nurse to every sick woman and child. A seamstress extraordinaire, she was also a cook whose delicacies were the highlight of every party on Officers Row, and whose tamales warmed the bellies of the enlisted men, providing a comfortable income for herself and her husband.

She saw my duffel bag. "Forgive me, *señor*, but I no do the enlisted soldier his laundry any more. Now I wash only for the officers and their wives. I have not time for anything else."

"I haven't come for my laundry. I've come for information."

With one hand, she held her veil in place against the wind. "Eenformation? What kind of eenformation?"

We were alone out here — it was as good a spot to talk as any. I showed her ten dollars. "The personal kind."

Her dark eyes moved from the ten dollars to me.

I added another ten.

She reached for the money, but I pulled it back. "This information is strictly between you and me. You won't ask why I want it, and you're to forget I was ever here."

"Very well."

I handed her the money. She unbuttoned her coat and slipped the greenbacks inside a frilly pink blouse that did not go with her swarthy complexion. "Twenty dollars is much money, *señor*. You must want this eenformation very badly."

"Like I said — that's my affair. Do you know Bucko Doyle, a private in I Company?"

"*Sí*, I know him. Everyone know him." She resumed hanging the underwear, clumping down the line while I followed behind.

"He has a friend who lives next door to you."

"Keetty Daugherty. *Sí*."

"He visits her after Lights Out?"

"*Sí*."

"A lot?"

"*Sí*. Yes. He is not the only one, of course. Keety, she is very popular."

"Was Doyle with Kitty Daugherty on the night of December 6?"

Mrs. Nash stopped. The wind made the taut clothesline sing; the drying underclothes flapped accompaniment. "*Señor*, I do not keep a calendar of this Doyle's visits. How would I — "

"It was the night that Lieutenant Redington was killed."

Her dark eyes widened. "Oh, I see." She thought for a second. "*Sí*. He was there. I remember. I always know when he is there. You hear them laughing. Then they drink too much and fight. Always it is the same."

"You're sure about that? That he was there?"

"Pretty sure. *Sí*."

"Any idea how long?"

"A while, I think. But it has been weeks now, I am no certain. I would not remember at all, except that all of us we were so shocked when Mister Redington died. It makes you remember what you were doing when you hear about it. What you were doing before that, too."

"Thanks," I told her, and I started away.

"That is all?" Mrs. Nash asked, incredulous.

"That's all."

"Then thank you," she said with a slight curtsy. "*Gracias*."

I stopped. "By the way, Mrs. Nash, why do you wear that veil?"

She batted her eyes coquettishly. "I must. The doctor says. The prairie wind, it is bad for a girl's complexion."

Mrs. Nash was hardly a girl. I guessed she was about my age. Still, that was her business. Behind me, two women were coming our way, lugging a huge bucket of wash to be hung up. "I am sorry that I could not help with your laundry, *señor*," Mrs. Nash said for their benefit as I left.

I dropped off my laundry at another house on the Row and started back to the barracks. The trumpeters were blowing "Recall From Fatigue." If I could get through the rest of the day without being shot at, beaten, or stabbed, I anticipated an interesting night at the Custers' house.

CHAPTER 18

"I'll take a glass of that lemonade," said Tom Custer.

We were in the huge parlor of his brother's house. I poured some of the lemonade, which was made from citric acid crystals—the Custers didn't allow liquor in their house. My job for the evening was to serve this stuff, then gather and clean the glasses. For this I was being paid five dollars. But I hadn't drawn this detail because I could mix lemonade. I was here to report what I'd learned to General Custer.

And what had I learned? That Bucko Doyle was Lieutenant Redington's killer. He had the victim's watch, which now rested in the pocket of my starched white jacket. But *was* Doyle the killer? I still wasn't certain.

Brother Tom, as Libby Custer called him, tasted his drink, looking at me with that aggressive arrogance peculiar to the Custers. On his uniform breast were two Medals of Honor. He had been one of three men to accomplish this feat during the war, earning the medals within a few days of each other in 1864. General Jackass did not have a Medal of Honor, and was supposedly jealous of Tom because of it.

Tom leaned forward and spoke in a lowered voice, so that no one else at the party could hear. "Armstrong says you're wasting our money. If it wasn't for Libby, we'd have sent you packing by now. We should never have hired anyone recommended by Wild Bill Hickok." He spoke the name with a sneer. "The great hero. Why, I personally ran that coward out of Hays City."

"That's not the way Bill tells it." I polished some glasses and set them on my serving table, which was made from sawhorses and boards. The tablecloth was a wagon cover, with "U.S." stenciled in the middle. "Bill says he arrested you for being drunk and shooting up the town. In retaliation you set five men on him, with orders to kill him. He only left town after he shot a couple of them, and the rest of your boys got up a lynching party."

Brother Tom's pale cheeks flushed crimson. "Hickok's a liar," he hissed.

"About some things, I agree."

It was all Tom could do to restrain himself. "I'll take you outside right now and whip you."

"You going to bring five men with you?" I asked.

Tom turned on his heel and joined the crowd of officers and their wives. A Christmas "tree" fashioned from sage and cedar brush hung from the parlor ceiling. The tree was adorned with paper decorations and festoons, with nuts wrapped in silver foil, ancient Christmas cards, bits of faded ribbon, and red candle stubs. Similar festoons and wreaths decorated the walls.

Every officer on the post was there, save the Officer of the Day. They had coalesced into three groups. One group consisted of close associates of General Custer—men like Myles Keogh, Lieutenant Cooke, and Captain Weir of D Company. A second centered around the dark, pasty-faced senior major, Marcus Reno. The third, men like Verity's friend Reed Granville and Lieutenant Porter, wandered between the other two. A few of the officers, like Tom Custer, wore regulation uniform, but since this was not a formal affair, most wore undress uniform of their own design. Lacking insignia, these getups were only identifiable as military by their blue color. Keogh and Myles Moylan, the gallantly mustachioed captain of A Company, wore shell jackets with waistcoats and bow ties (Keogh's tie was emerald green); others wore suit jackets or cutaway coats with tails. Lieutenant Wallace had a neck-high coat with elaborate frogging around the buttons, and Edgerly wore a double-breasted affair with rows of gilt buttons on its velvet lapels.

The ladies grouped around Libby Custer, who was entertaining a house guest from her home town in Michigan. This young woman, an intelligent-looking blonde, was saying, "I understand your husband goes next year to drive the Indians from the Yellowstone Valley and open it for the Northern Pacific Railroad."

Libby stared at her guest like the young woman had just advocated devil worship.

"That's what they say back in the States," the young woman explained, taken aback.

"No, no. Nothing could be further from the truth," Libby told her. "General Custer goes in the cause of justice. We have tried to be fair with the Indians, but they possess an undying hatred for the white man, and their chiefs, while pretending friendship for the army and settlers, secretly encourage their young followers to perpetrate murder, arson, and — dare I say it — rapine. The government has no choice. The guilty Indians must be punished and the rest confined within the agencies. An ultimatum has been issued. In defiance, Sitting Bull, the wiliest chief of all, and a great coward, has summoned all the tribes which pay him tribute to the Powder River country, and now General Custer must go there and teach them a lesson."

She stopped and turned. "Charlotte, be a dear, will

you, and bring us another plate of that hardtack and buffaloberry jam."

This last was spoken to Mrs. Moylan. "Of course, Elizabeth," said Mrs. Moylan.

The hardtack, along with ham sandwiches, formed the party's principal food. Libby's young guest ground her teeth into a piece of the tack. "It's fascinating, the way you officers make do out here on the frontier, Mrs. Custer. But what about the enlisted men? How do they live? What do they eat?"

"The men live extremely well. Every soldier in our regiment is a perfect physical specimen. And as for food, why, their ration is so large that a man who can eat it all in a day is renowned as a glutton."

I was wondering if maybe there was another regiment I didn't know about, when from the door came cries of "Here's the man of the hour," and "Happy birthday, King."

Lieutenant Arthur Manley, whom everyone called "King," entered, accompanied by his wife, Evangeline. Manley was a sour-looking fellow, only a year or two younger than General Custer. His trouser legs bore the blue stripe of the foot soldier — he commanded a company of the Twentieth Infantry, whose main duty was to provide garrison security when the Seventh was in the field.

Manley's wife was pretty and vivacious, but there were wrinkles around her eyes and mouth, and no amount of elaborate combing could conceal the first touches of gray in her dark hair. Her eyes met mine across the room. I looked away, but not before I felt a tingle, the kind you get when you know a woman is available. I could picture her growing older in this godforsaken place, feeling frustrated and unloved. It was not difficult for that kind of woman to get into trouble. Maybe keeping an eye on her helped account for her husband's sour disposition. Manley joined Reno's group, while his wife moved in among the other ladies, jostling for a place close to Mrs. Custer.

So far, General Custer had not been seen—he was shy and left Libby in charge of the social arrangements; but he made an appearance when the cake was brought out by Mrs. Nash, who was done up in pink furze, still wearing her veil. The cake was greeted with applause, and Custer said, "Many happy returns of the day, Arthur. Our Aztec princess used the last of the eggs from St. Paul to make this for you. I'm sure it's excellent, as her creations always are."

Mrs. Nash curtsied and batted her large eyes.

Custer joined in singing "For He's the Jolly Good Fellow," then retreated once more to his library. When the cake had been devoured, the tables were pushed aside and the carpet—made from blankets edged with calico—was rolled up. Lieutenant Edgerly sat at the piano, another officer produced a banjo, yet another a jew's harp. Partners were chosen and the dancing began.

The floor was a color-splashed swirl of silks and taffetas, most of them five to ten years out of date. Mrs. Custer's young guest was the woman most in demand, followed by Libby herself and Evangeline Manley. Demand for the few other women was not far behind, as the officers eagerly awaited turns.

Breathing hard, Mrs. Custer took a break from the dancing. She looked on approvingly while her protégé was whirled round by a succession of officers. "How's the prospective bride doing?" I heard Charlotte Moylan ask her.

"She seems to be enjoying herself," Libby said. "Not like the last one. I pray she has her head turned by one of these young men and marries him. I like to get the bachelor officers married off. It makes for a happier regiment. Much less temptation." She cast a sour glance at Mrs. Manley, who essayed a polka with dashing Myles Keogh, while her husband looked on glumly.

The impromptu orchestra struck up "Garry Owen" in waltz time. At that moment the duty orderly appeared at the door with a note. Clearing his throat, the orderly handed the note to Libby. Libby read the note and clasped a hand to her breast. "The General commands me to join him in the library for a waltz," she announced. Gathering her skirts, she hurried off.

Nearby, Major Reno slapped Manley on the shoulder. "Let's go outside for cigars, shall we? Don't want the smoke to disturb the ladies."

These two, along with Lieutenants Erickson, Granville, and Sturgis, bowed to the ladies and trooped outside. I picked up a tray, under the pretense of collecting glasses to be washed. Unseen, I slipped out the back door and onto the piazza, as Mrs. Custer called it. Erickson, Manley, and Granville were the three men who had known Redington best. I wanted to hear what they had to say.

CHAPTER 19

I hid behind the corner of the porch, ignoring the bitter cold, listening.

There was the rasp of matches, brief flares of light, the harsh smell of cigars borne away on the wind. Then came the soft plop of a cork. I chanced a look. Major Reno had opened a whiskey bottle that he must have concealed out there before going into the party.

"Here, Jack," Reno said. "Take a nip." Jack was Jack Sturgis, son of Colonel Sam Sturgis, who was the Seventh's actual commander. Sturgis was kept on recruiting duty back east by General Sheridan, so that Custer, Sheridan's protégé, could lead the outfit. Jack had just joined the Seventh, fresh from the Point. He was spending Christmas at Lincoln before joining his company at Fort Totten.

"It's all right," Reno assured him. "Have some hardtack and jam when you go back in, to hide your breath. You'll be fine as long as you don't pass out or throw up on Mrs. Custer."

The four officers arranged themselves on the porch rail, smoking, handing the bottle back and forth, while I remained hidden in the shadows. Reed Granville said, "How do you like the Seventh so far, Jacky?"

Young Sturgis paused, framing his words. "It's not what I expected. I put in for the Seventh to be with my father. General and Mrs. Custer have been more than kind to me, but it's plain they don't want my father around. No one even acknowledges that my father commands the regiment."

"Custer certainly don't acknowledge it," Reno cracked. "Speaking of our valiant leader, I hear he plans to be at the Centennial Exposition in Philadelphia on July 4, with his whole tribe."

"Guess he ain't planning on a long campaign," Erickson said wryly. "Somebody better tell Sitting Bull." Erickson was a spare, athletic fellow who combed his blond hair straight back. The sharp planes of his face looked like they'd been slabbed on with a putty knife.

Reno went on. "He's hoping to be in Philadelphia with the Democratic presidential nomination in hand."

There was a hush. "Do you think he can get it?" asked Manley.

"If we win him a big victory, it's possible," Reno said. Then he chuckled. "Can you picture Custer as president? How long do you think it would take him to get us into a war?"

"About six months," Erickson guessed. "How long do you think it would take him to lose it?"

"About six months. He'd have to command the army, of course."

"Of course," said Erickson. "No point in having the war, otherwise."

Reed Granville intervened. "I don't like to hear the General spoken of this way. He's a fine soldier."

"He's a terrible soldier," Erickson said. "Hasn't the foggiest idea how to command."

Reno said, "He doesn't consult his officers, doesn't tell anyone what he's doing, or why. Everything's a big secret. The only thing he knows how to do is attack. It's a miracle he didn't get killed during the war, with some of those hare-brained stunts he pulled. He got enough of his men killed, that's for certain."

"He almost got the whole Seventh Cavalry killed on the Washita," Erickson said.

Jack Sturgis sounded puzzled, "I thought the Washita was a great victory."

"That's what everybody thinks, who wasn't there. We charged into that village without reconnoitering. And that was after Custer had split the regiment in four. Turned out there were a couple thousand more redskins camped just upstream. If those Indians had attacked, not a man of us would have lived to tell the tale. It was only by a ruse we got out alive—and California Joe, the scout, came up with that. Bloody luck, is what it was."

"Luck is Custer's god," Reno said. "He counts on it. Thinks it's a substitute for tactical ability. Sooner or later, though, luck runs out." He paused and drew on his cigar. "I just don't want to be there when he has a bad day."

There was muffled agreement from Erickson and Manley. Another bottle was opened. "I can't believe we're talking about the same man," Granville said. I could picture his rugged face glowering at the others the way he'd glowered at me when he saw me with Verity Winslow. "General Custer was an idol to us younger officers during the war. Gettysburg, Brandy Station, Aldie—his deeds were a byword for daring and courage."

"They were a byword for stupidity," Erickson said.

Reno puffed his cigar thoughtfully. "Custer's problem is that he still thinks of himself as the 'Boy General.' He doesn't seem to realize that he's no longer a boy—and no longer a general."

Granville's voice rose a notch. "You won't deny there's no braver man in the army."

"Know what makes him that way?" Erickson said. "He can't get it up. Uses fighting as a substitute. Always has. Why do you think he and Libby don't have any kids? That's why he deserted the regiment to be with her in '67. He finally got a hard on."

Reno shook his head. "He got it up with those darkie maids that he and Libby had in Virginia—that's what everybody said. And what about that Cheyenne princess he kept for the winter after the Washita? He gave her a baby."

"Was it him," responded Erickson, "or Brother Tom? They both had her, you know."

Manley had another opinion. "I hear he's got the clap. That's why he looks so old. It's why he doesn't go near Libby, too—he doesn't want her to get it. Niggers and Injuns he doesn't care about. He's so brave because he knows the clap's going to kill him anyway."

Granville said, "Don't listen to this horse pizzle, Jacky. General Custer is an excellent soldier. A lot of people are simply jealous of him. I sometimes think there's officers in this command—no one present, of course—who hate General Custer so much, they'd let him die before they'd go to help him."

"Why shouldn't they?" said Erickson vehemently. "That's what he did to Joel Elliot. Abandoned him and nineteen men at the Washita. We found 'em later, what was left of 'em. The son of a bitch. I can forgive him a lot, but not that. Joel was a good man, a good officer."

"Everyone knows he had no choice but to leave those men," Granville countered. "The command was in imminent danger. To have remained would have been folly."

"Really? You don't think he'd have left Brother Tom,

do you? Or Jimmy Calhoun? He'd have stayed for them no matter how many lives it cost."

Reno laughed, easing the tension. "All right, you two. Calm down."

Erickson got in a last shot. "Reed, you're starting to sound like Tom Weir — or Peter Redington."

"Redington," Manley growled. "Getting rid of him was the best thing we ever did."

"*We* did?" said Jack Sturgis, who sounded like he'd had too much to drink.

"Figure of speech, Jacky. What I meant was, some public-spirited individual got rid of him for us." He hoisted the bottle. "Here's to the fellow, whoever he is."

Erickson said, "I'm just glad I got my money back from the bastard before whoever it was bonkered him."

"How much did he owe you?" Reno asked.

"Just short of three hundred dollars."

Reno whistled. "That's a lot. Where'd he get it?"

"Damned if I know — or care. I told him I'd see him run him out of the service if he didn't pay. I would have, too. Gambling debts are a matter of honor."

Reno said, "Sorry, Reed, I know Redington was a friend of yours. You must think we're ganging up on you tonight."

Granville said, "I don't think a lot of you ever really gave Peter a chance. He wasn't as bad a fellow as everyone makes him out to be." Then he added, "Anyway, you're just a bunch of drunken malcontents."

There was some good-natured jostling and laughter, then Erickson said, "You knew Redington at the Point, didn't you, Jack?"

"We were in the same class," young Sturgis replied. "He had a reputation as a snob — which was funny, because he didn't have any money."

Reno snorted. "Nothing changed when he got here. He snubbed Myles Moylan because Myles had been a ranker, wouldn't talk to him outside of duty—and Myles a captain. I heard him refer to Charlotte as 'a washerwoman' once. Libby liked him, though, and that's what counts."

Jack went on. "He didn't get many demerits, as I recall. Most of them were for gambling—though once he was caught bringing a woman into the barracks, a shopkeeper's
... wife ... from town."

His voice tailed off as he realized what he was saying, and there was an uncomfortable silence. No one voiced Evangeline Manley's name, but she was on their minds.

At last Reno cleared his throat. "My smoke's about done. We'd better get inside before we're missed. Jacky's starting to look a little blue."

The officers rose and stretched. "Leave the bottles under the porch," Reno told them. "I'll collect them on my way out." He pitched his cigar butt into the darkness. There was a faint fizzing sound as it hit the snow.

As they were leaving, I slipped around the side of the house and through the back door. I took my tray of dirty glasses, made my way through the hall and into the noisy parlor, where I was stopped by Tom Custer.

"Where have you been?" Tom demanded.

"Detecting," I told him.

"Well, get a fresh tray of lemonade and detect yourself to the library. The General's waiting for you."

CHAPTER 20

I filled my tray with fresh glasses of lemonade and started for the parlor door. As I did, Evangeline Manley appeared in my path. "May I have some of that lemonade?"

"Help yourself, ma'am."

"I'm thirsty from the dancing."

"Yes, ma'am."

She sipped the bitter-tasting (there was no sugar for it) lemonade. She lifted her glass gingerly, as if the motion pained her. As she did, her ruffled sleeve rose up, and I noticed a deep purple bruise on her wrist, as if she'd been gripped very tightly and fingertips had dug into her flesh. Camouflaged by powder, the tip of an ugly welt peeked from her collar. "You're new, aren't you?" she asked.

The fact that an officer's wife noticed enlisted men was unusual. "Yes, ma'am. I've been in the regiment just about two weeks."

"You're older than the other men."

"Yes, ma'am."

"Are you new to the frontier?"

"No, ma'am. Born and raised west of the Mississippi."

She sighed. "You're accustomed to it, then. I don't think I ever will be. It's so big — so lonely."

"It's not exactly the Forest of Arden," I admitted.

Her violet eyes widened, and she looked at me directly for the first time. "You know the Bard?"

131

"A bit."

"How unusual. Perhaps—and I hope you won't think I'm being forward—we can discuss him some time. Conversation is so limited out here. All that army women talk about is their husbands' careers. All their husbands talk about is the same. It would be a rare treat to speak about a subject other than the promotion lists."

I shifted uncomfortably. "I don't think that's possible, ma'am. You're an officer's wife and I'm an enlisted man. They wouldn't allow it."

"No. I suppose they wouldn't. Life can be so unjust."

"I won't argue with you there. I'd better be going. General Custer is waiting for this lemonade."

"I'm sorry. I didn't mean to detain you."

"It was my pleasure, ma'am."

She returned to the dancing. I felt sorry for her. There was an almost desperate quality about her. She must have been easy pickings for a ladies man like Peter Redington. Once again, I started for the parlor door.

"Barman!"

I turned to see Lieutenant Manley coming toward me, square features clouded. "What were you talking to my wife about?" he demanded in a low voice.

I stood at semi-attention, eyes fixed in the middle distance. "Shakespeare, sir."

"Don't give me that," he said, and he added, "I know who you are."

"Really?" I kept my eyes fixed in that middle distance, inwardly cursing Keogh's big mouth. In a low voice, I said, "In that case, perhaps won't mind me asking—did you finish the job on Lieutenant Redington, like you threatened?"

Manley's face turned white, then red. "Who told you

about that?"

"Does it matter?"

"Was it Evangeline?"

"No. And you haven't answered the question."

He looked around, to see if anyone was watching us. No one was. "No, I didn't finish the job," he growled. "I admit, I was going to, but I thought better of it and returned to my quarters."

"Any witnesses?"

"Only my wife."

"Were you and Redington fighting about your wife or about the way you treat her?"

Manley's brow clouded again. "I've heard enough from you. Keep away from Evangeline, do you understand?"

I turned, and I fixed my eyes on his. "And if I don't? What are you going to do—give her another beating?"

He nearly took a swing at me in front of everybody. Then he got control of himself. "You've been warned," he hissed.

"I've been warned before. Plenty of times. Now, if you'll excuse me." I slipped by, leaving him to fume.

I rapped on the library door and was told to come in.

Custer was there, in full dress uniform, pacing back and forth. Libby stood beside him, along with Brother Tom, Myles Keogh with his green tie, and Lieutenant Cooke, the adjutant, dundrearies flowing down his chest. Blucher and another dog were curled on the couch. The mouse was in its inkwell, asleep.

Custer ceased pacing. Like everything he did, there was a flourish to the act. "Good evening, Mister Hughes."

The overhead light shone through his thinning hair. On his shoulder pads, two silver leaves denoted his actual rank, lieutenant colonel.

"Good evening, General." I set down the tray. Keogh and Cooke picked up glasses.

"Took your time getting here," Custer said.

"I was delayed." From habit, I almost added, "sir." I was starting to think like a soldier.

"Let's get to the point. What have you learned?"

I took Redington's silver watch from the pocket of my white jacket and handed it to him. There were mutters of recognition as he opened the watch and showed it to the others. "Where did you find this?"

"In Bucko Doyle's mattress."

"Good work, Hughes," said Cooke, examining the watch.

Libby beamed. "You see, Autie, I told you he'd find the guilty man."

Custer looked at Keogh. "Who's Doyle?"

"A private in my company, General."

"Get the Sergeant of the Guard and arrest him."

Keogh started for the door.

"Wait," I said.

Keogh paused. The others looked at me.

"I'm not certain Doyle is the killer."

"What?" said Tom.

"Don't be ridiculous," Keogh added. "We have a witness who heard Doyle threaten Redington's life. We have the dead man's watch in Doyle's possession. What more do you want?"

"Something about it doesn't feel right." To Keogh, I said, "How long has Doyle been in the army?"

Keogh thought. "A bit over three years."

"A hard case like that, in three years he must have been bucked and gagged a dozen times. So why does he pick this time to kill the officer who ordered it?"

Keogh shrugged. "He'd just had enough, I suppose. He snapped."

"I doubt a man like Doyle ever gets enough."

Cooke said, "Maybe he had a particular dislike for this officer."

"Maybe, but Redington hadn't been with the company long. The dislike would have to have built up in one hell of a—excuse me, ma'am, one heck—of a hurry."

Custer looked at me shrewdly, flipping the watch case open and closed in the palm of his hand. "What are you suggesting? How else could this watch have come into Doyle's possession?"

"It could have been planted."

"By whom?" said Cooke. "Another member of the company?"

"Maybe. Or maybe Redington's killer wasn't an enlisted man, at all. Maybe he was an officer."

This remark produced an outburst. "Don't be ridiculous," sneered Tom.

"That's the stupidest thing I ever heard," Keogh said.

Libby Custer spoke, and her voice managed to be both soothing and condescending at the same time. "I don't believe that Mr. Hughes understands the army. Officers are gentlemen and, as such, men of honor. They are incapable of murder."

"Really, ma'am? Did you know that Redington was having an affair with the wife of another officer at this post? Don't you think that's a motive for murder?"

The men in the room looked at one another uncomfortably. Libby stiffened in shock, then recovered, inclining her head like a schoolmistress addressing a stubborn child. "The army is a family, Mr. Hughes. Such occurrences as the one you describe are best handled within the family. We can't allow anything that would damage the reputation of General Custer or his regiment. I repeat, an officer could not have committed this crime."

Custer agreed. "I'm satisfied that this Doyle is the killer."

"I'm not," I said.

"So what is it you want?"

"More time."

"More time," said Tom, "or more money? Are you sure you just don't want to sit around and enjoy Christmas at my brother's expense?"

In a deceptively soft voice Libby added, "I agree with Colonel Tom, Mr. Hughes—this request for more time seems like a ploy to pad your bill."

"Beg your pardon, ma'am, but I don't pad my bills. And even if I did, this is the last place in the world I'd want to spend Christmas."

"So why don't you leave?" Custer said. "You've got no personal stake in this."

"I take pride in my work, General. I don't like Bucko Doyle, but I don't want him to hang for something he didn't do. As a man of honor, I wouldn't think you'd want that, either."

Custer and Libby looked at each other for a long moment. They seemed able to communicate without words. Then Custer said to me, "I'll give you till Christmas."

"That's only two days."

"It's all you'll get. Mrs. Custer and I leave for the States after the New Year. I want this wrapped up before we go. I plan to lay the framework for my presidential bid on this trip, and I don't want embarrassments cropping up in my rear. If you haven't come up with a more credible suspect, we'll arrest Private Doyle and charge him with Redington's murder."

"But—"

"No 'but's'. That's it." He looked around the room. "Is there anything else?"

No one spoke.

"Very well. Gentlemen, you may return and enjoy the party."

Keogh opened the door; the music from the ball room got louder. He, Tom Custer, and Cooke left. I got the lemonade tray and started out the door after them.

"Mr. Hughes—a moment, if you please."

I stopped.

"Shut the door."

I did. The room quieted once more. "Hughes, I'm curious," said Custer. "The last time we talked, you told me you'd killed four men in cold blood. I was hoping you might explain."

I put down the tray. "I was orphaned by an Indian raid when I was two. I was found by a party of minute men, led by our neighbor, Sixtus Danville. The Danvilles took me in, raised me as one of their own. They had a daughter, Lydia. Lydia was the same age as me. We grew up together. At some point we became more than friends. We planned to marry."

I wiped my hands down my trouser legs; this wasn't something I liked to remember. It was also something I never forgot. "Then the war came, and I . . . I left home. When I came back, Sixtus and his family had lost their land to Yankee carpetbaggers. While they were on the road, looking for a new place to live, they ran into four horse thieves. The thieves robbed the Danvilles of what little remained to them, and when they left, they took Lydia with them. Sixtus found her later. She had been . . . she had been raped. Then murdered."

I stopped again. Words could never express the pain I had felt when I'd heard, the guilt I had felt — still felt — for coming back late from the war, even though it hadn't been my fault. Something wet rolled down my cheek, and through the mist I saw Lydia again as she had been in our younger days — blonde and beautiful, laughing and full of life.

"I tracked down those four men, and I killed them. No regrets."

"Why didn't you resort to the law?" Libby asked.

"The only law in Texas in those days was the Yankee military courts. Those horse thieves were Yanks, I was a Rebel. They'd have gotten off. Besides, I wanted to kill them myself. I wanted the satisfaction. I enjoyed it."

"And then what?"

"Then I left Texas. I was wanted for murder there. Still am, though I go back from time to time, to look for my sister, Becky, who was kidnapped in that Indian raid."

"But if you're caught, you'll be hanged," Libby said.

"That's a chance I'll take."

"Where did this outrage to your young lady occur?" Custer asked.

"Crockett County."

He stiffened. "Then those military courts you were so afraid of using were under my jurisdiction."

"I know."

"It occurs to me that you're not much different than the men you're hired to bring to justice."

"I've been told that before."

Custer gave me a sour look. "You have two days to produce the killer. Otherwise, we arrest Doyle."

"You'll have your man," I promised. But I did not feel nearly as confident as I sounded.

CHAPTER 21

Verity Winslow was waiting in front of McKenzie's Theater, as I had instructed her, greeting the stares of passing men with haughty disdain. Nobody could get her nose in the air like Verity.

"Where have you been?" she said, blowing on her hands to warm them. "I've been waiting here over an hour. It's freezing. I was getting ready to go home."

"It's not that easy to sneak off post. I had to wait till everyone was asleep. Then I had to dodge the guards." Once again, I'd had the feeling I was being followed as I came into town, but this time I chalked it up to my imagination. "Let's go somewhere warm."

We crossed the street to Lucky Leo's restaurant. It was Christmas Eve. The place was packed; everyone was laughing and happy. It smelled of wet wool, unwashed bodies, and frying food. The unfinished pine floor was streaked with mud from the patrons' boots and shoes. We got a table and Verity, who hadn't eaten, ordered a steak and potatoes. The potatoes, rare as an honest lawyer at this time of year, cost as much as the steak. I was supposed to be broke, so I contented myself with coffee. I slumped in my chair, pouring the hot, black liquid into myself while Verity waited for her food.

"You look tired, Mister Hughes."

"I had water detail, I was chopping ice all morning. I had extra duty the last two nights, and I was here the night before that. I could use some sleep. Did you get that information I asked for?"

"Yes, I did, thank you very much. I can see why you wanted someone else to do the work—it cost me two weeks' pay in telegraph charges."

"And?"

"And . . . your companies don't exist."

"What?"

"Sioux City Cattle and Missouri Valley Grains—they don't exist."

"You're kidding."

"I wish I was. I wouldn't have had to look so hard for them if they were real. They aren't listed on the Chicago Exchange, or any other. I couldn't find any banking or tax records for them, no mailing addresses, no deeds of incorporation. Companies that big, there would have to be records. Mr. Lounsberry's upset because I've been neglecting my other duties. I told him that he'll understand when he sees my story. I just hope there is a story."

I stroked my lower lip in thought. "Haselmere's up to something. But what's it got to do with Redington?"

"Nothing that I can see," Verity said.

"Then why did Haselmere's shoulder hitters warn you off the Redington story?"

She shrugged and shook her head.

Verity's food came. You might think I'd have been sick of beef by now, but this was pan-fried steak with gravy, not the stringy stuff we had in the mess hall. I eyed it the same way a starving dog would, but Verity didn't notice. She had a healthy appetite. "I've done my part," she said between bites. "Now tell me what you've found out."

I related all that I'd learned since we'd last met,

including my suspicion that Redington's watch might have been planted in Bucko Doyle's mattress. A stunned look came over Verity's face while I was talking. She stopped eating; her usual ebullience became strangely subdued.

"What's wrong?" I asked her.

"Nothing. I was just—I wonder if Arthur Manley could have planted the watch. I always thought he might be beating Evangeline, but I couldn't be certain."

"But if Manley killed Redington, who busted that shot at me up on the Heart River? Manley couldn't have gotten away from the post for that long."

"Maybe he's partners with someone in your company. Maybe they set up Doyle together."

"I doubt it. Interaction between officers and men of the same company is infrequent enough. Between officers and men of different companies, it's almost non-existent. Plus, Manley's infantry, which makes it even more unlikely."

"Then maybe the incidents are unrelated. You're not all that likeable, you know. I could picture busting a shot or two at you myself."

"That's comforting to hear. Perhaps you could also picture where Redington got the money to pay back Lieutenant Erickson. And while you're at it, see if you can picture what any of that has to do with Haselmere."

Again Verity had no answer. She picked at her meal, but ate no more. Her appetite seemed to have deserted her.

"Did you move into that abandoned cottage?" I asked.

"What? That's right—I'd forgotten you were there when we discussed it. Yes, I did. It's more than satisfactory—much better than Mrs. Crosbie's boarding house. Sitting Bull loves it—barks at anything that comes within a hundred yards of the place. I feel quite safe with him there."

"Where's your boyfriend tonight?"

"Reed? At the post. He says he's required to spend a certain amount of time with the other officers at the club. Is that right?"

I nodded. "It's supposed to build *esprit de corps*."

"If he just wasn't a soldier . . ," she sighed. Then she stopped. "What are you gawking at?"

I stared out the window. "Guess who just walked by on the other side of the street?"

"Santa Claus?"

"Even better—Amos Haselmere."

Verity craned her neck to look.

I rose, gulping the rest of my coffee. "Let's see what he's up to."

Verity followed, leaving the remains of her meal. I looked at the steak. "Do you mind?"

She made a dismissive gesture. "Suit yourself."

I picked up the steak and started for the door. I opened it and started through, but Verity cleared her throat from behind. I stopped, stepped aside, and held the door for her, bowing as she went past. She dipped her head in acknowledgment, and we made our way across the churned-up bog that was Main Street, dodging the Christmas Eve crowd in pursuit of Haselmere.

CHAPTER 22

For a short, stocky man, Haselmere moved with surprising speed. I kept my eye on the fur collar of his astrakhan, as I trailed him along the icy sidewalk. I bounced off people, ignoring their muttered remonstrances. Verity kept pace with me. The frigid air was redolent with the smell of wood smoke from stoves. Down the street, a group of Christmas carolers was singing, occasionally firing pistols in accompaniment.

I chewed on the steak as I went, tearing off hunks of it, the gravy dripping down my fingers and over my hand. "Really, Mister Hughes," said Verity, "your manners are atrocious. What else do you do—drink water from puddles?"

"I can tell you've never been in Texas," I replied. "There's times I've been glad to see a good puddle."

Just then, Haselmere entered the Tough Nut saloon. Verity and I stopped outside. "Wait out here," I told her. "I'll go in. You'd attract too much attention."

As I opened one of the glass-paneled doors, Verity slid in ahead of me. "You're not keeping me out," she said.

"But—"

Too late. She plunged through the crowd. I popped the rest of the steak in my mouth and hurried after, licking gravy off my fingers.

We inched our way across the saloon, stepping over vomit puddles on the sawdust floor. Startled at seeing a female face, men pressed around us. "You Konrad's new girl?" growled a fellow in a battered plug hat and buckskins. Tobacco drooled from the side of his mouth and down his beard. He reached for Verity's waist. " 'Bout time we got us a decent-looking whore in this shit hole."

Verity slapped the offending hand aside. "I beg your pardon. I am not a companion for hire. And I'll thank you to watch your language."

Irate, Tobacco Drool started after her, but I stopped him. "Leave her be," I told him. "Believe me, she's more trouble than she's worth."

His brow knit, and for a moment I thought I'd have to fight him, but the press of the crowd carried me away.

I caught up with Verity. Ahead of us, Haselmere opened a door and went into the back room.

Verity and I stopped. We couldn't go in there. I grabbed her hand. "Come on," I told her. We pushed back out of the saloon to a chorus of protests.

"Now that you're here, honey, stay awhile." It was Tobacco Drool, swaggering into our path. His huge hand swatted me out of the way as effortlessly as if I had been a fly. "Let's you and me go upstairs," he told Verity with a blast of whiskey breath. "I can make it last all night."

Verity looked him up and down. "If you could make it last ten seconds, I'd be surprised."

Tobacco Drool deflated as though somebody had stuck a pin in him, while the men around him laughed. "Now stand aside," Verity commanded.

Dumbfounded, he did.

"Told you," I said to him as I went past.

Outside again, I led Verity around the side of the Tough Nut. "What—?" she began.

"Sh-h-h." I put a finger to my lips. We entered the alley behind the building. The alley was used as a public latrine, and even in the bitter cold, the stench was overwhelming. "Watch where you put your feet," I whispered.

"Too late," Verity replied.

As I'd hoped, there was a window in the building's rear. A light shone from inside. Verity and I crept up to the window, which was closed because of the cold. Muted voices could be heard through the glass. We peeped over the sill. The glass was so dirty, it was like looking through the bottom of a beer bottle, but I made out Haselmere's astrakhan and oily hair as he warmed his hands next to the stove. At the table beside him sat an ugly man with a sulfurous face and a red beard that looked like it had exploded out of his chin.

"That's Schofield," I whispered to Verity. "Indian agent from Standing Rock."

They were talking to a third man, who was out of sight, off to one side by the window. I twisted my head to see.

The soft pine window frame exploded next to my eyes, splinters gouging my cheek and forehead. At the same instant, I heard the gunshot. I flung Verity and myself aside as another shot split the darkness. Inside, the back room erupted with curses and shouting. I jerked Verity to her feet. "Come on!"

We ran down the dark alley. Behind us was the crack of another shot. Something droned past my ear. The alley was full of trash—abandoned crates, wagon wheels, a dead cat. There were thumping footsteps just behind us. Heavy breathing. An oath, as one of our pursuers hit something. At the same time I tripped and went headlong, sliding in the frozen ooze. I scrambled up, helped by Verity, as another pistol shot exploded nearby.

They were bound to catch us. In her dress and high heels, Verity wasn't fast enough to outrun them. I was unarmed, and there was no hope for outside help—the shots would go unnoticed amidst the Christmas revelry. We came to a narrow passageway between two buildings, and I pushed Verity into it.

"Keep going," I told her, and I turned and dropped into a crouch.

A tall shadow loomed in the passageway as the first of our pursuers made the turn into it. I lunged at him, driving my shoulder into his waist, knocking him onto his back and going for his pistol. He cursed, and I got a whiff of foul-smelling breath. The other man came up from behind.

"Shoot him!" cried my man.

"*Merde*—I cannot see!"

We wrestled in the icy mud. I tried to pry the pistol from my man's strong grasp, but couldn't. Something metallic slammed into the side of my head. I was momentarily paralyzed, my fingers went numb.

I heard the click of a pistol hammer beside my ear.

I was going to die.

There was a flash, a sharp crack, a grunt. The gun barrel fell away from my ear.

Above me there was an oath in French, and a shot went I didn't know where. I willed my uncoordinated hands to reach for the wounded man's pistol. I pulled it away from him, rolled onto my back, and fired at the dark shadow looming over me. In the flash I saw a beard with a white streak down the center. The shadow went down, as if pulled by unseen hands. The wounded man beside me came at me again. Before I could react, there was another shot from the passageway. The man fell on top of me and lay still.

I heaved the man aside and scrambled unsteadily to my feet. My head throbbed. I was dizzy. I turned to see who had saved me. It was Verity. In her hand was a short-barreled .38 Colt.

Down the alley, from the direction of the Tough Nut, angry voices were coming closer. "Let's go," I told Verity. I pushed her back into the passageway, tossing my assailant's pistol from my hand as I did.

We exited the passageway and joined the throngs on Main Street, where the carolers continued singing and shooting. Verity and I walked away as calmly as we could, though people stared at my light blue overcoat, which was covered with mire and with blood from the man who'd fallen on me.

"Why didn't you tell me you had a gun?" I said to Verity.

"You didn't ask," she said. "After that evening at the Point, do you think I'd let myself be assaulted again with impunity?"

I shook my head. "The government doesn't need Custer and the Seventh. They should just send you after Sitting Bull."

The surge of energy that comes in desperate situations was still flowing through me. I wanted to run, to fight, to do something. It was starting to wear off Verity, though, and shock was setting in. Her step faltered. "You were prepared to die to save me, weren't you?" she asked.

The question made me uneasy, and I shrugged.

"You would have died, if I hadn't had the pistol."

"I had to do something," I told her. "You were too slow and clumsy to get away from those two."

"Clumsy!" Her green eyes flashed. "It was you that fell down, not me." She paused. This was hard for her. "Anyway—thank you."

"Forget it. Fortunately, the debt is paid."

"Yes. I—I never shot a man before."

"If you're lucky, you'll never have to shoot another. It's not as much fun as the dime novels make it out to be."

"Do you think they're dead?"

"I'm not going back to see, I can tell you that." I threw a look over my shoulder, but no one was coming after us.

Verity said, "It was the two men who attacked me before, wasn't it?"

I nodded. "St. Jacques and Whitehead. They were trying to kill me, this time. I don't know if Haselmere's involved in Redington's death or not, but whatever he's up to, he'll go to any length to keep it quiet."

"How did they know we were there?"

"They must have been in the Tough Nut. They spotted us there, and we didn't notice. I wish we could have seen the third man in that room. I've got an idea his identity would answer a lot of questions."

A saloon door opened, momentarily bathing me in yellow light from inside. "Look at you," Verity said, "your uniform is a mess. I have some benzyne at my house. Let's see if we can get you cleaned up."

"I don't think you're safe, staying by yourself," I said as we slogged across the crowded street. "You should go back to Lounsberry's."

She laughed. "You sound like Reed." Then she realized something. "Oh, my God. Reed's going to go off like a Roman candle when he finds out what happened tonight."

"Are you going to tell him I was with you?"

"No. I don't want to get you in trouble—you do too a good job of that on your own. Maybe I shouldn't tell him about this at all. He doesn't like me exposing myself to danger. I can imagine what a fuss he'll make when I go on the campaign next spring."

"Still got your heart set on that, huh?"

"Of course. Why wouldn't I?"

"What is it you want, anyway? What drives you?"

"It's easy—I want to be the best. I want to be famous, like Mr. Stanley, finding Dr. Livingstone."

"If Livingstone saw you coming, he'd probably run the other way."

We were on a street of modest frame houses, most with picket fences. Somewhere nearby a group of Germans was singing "Silent Night" in their native language. The music drifted across the frosty air with its message of hope and joy. Ice and snow crunched beneath our feet. It was hard to believe that a few minutes ago someone had been trying to kill us.

"Right here," said Verity.

We stopped before a small cottage. I opened the gate. Something lay on the cottage's low doorstep.

"A package," Verity said. "Probably a Christmas present from Reed."

As she started forward, I put out my arm, stopping her. It was no package. It was an animal, and something dark was dripping from it, forming a pool on the icy walk.

Verity saw it now, too, and she clutched my arm, fingers digging into the heavy cloth of my overcoat.

I moved closer. It was the big yellow dog, Sitting Bull.

Someone had slit its throat.

Behind me, Verity gave a gasp of horror. I turned her away from the sight and pulled her close to me.

"Why would anyone hurt Sitting Bull?" she sobbed into my chest.

"It was another warning. Stay away from the Redington story. Or next time, it'll be you."

I held her at arm's length. "It's time we leveled with each other, Verity. I'm not really a soldier. I'm a detective, hired to find Redington's killer."

Her eyes searched out mine and held them. "I knew it," she said through her tears.

"Whoever killed Redington is willing to kill me to hide his tracks. He's willing to kill you, as well. Now you level with me. Who is your informant?"

She shuddered, let out her breath. "Very well," she said in a low voice not much above a whisper. "You know him. It's . . . it's Private Doyle."

CHAPTER 23

Christmas Day dawned bright and cold, the snowbound quiet broken only by the guards' cries of "All's well," and the distant tolling of a church bell in Bismarck.

I was too tired to care. I had been up most of the night. First I had buried the dog Sitting Bull, then Verity Winslow pulled the splinters from my forehead and cheek. "You're lucky you didn't lose an eye," she said, maneuvering her tweezers with all the deftness of a drunken surgeon. After that, Verity and I tried to get my uniform clean. We took brushes and benzyne to it and got out a lot of the blood and mud and God knows what else was on it, but it was still a mess. The work helped take Verity's mind off the killing of her dog.

I'd stumbled back to the fort with less than an hour till "Reveille." My eyelids felt like there were curtain weights hanging from them. There was no time for sleep, however. I had until tomorrow to produce Lieutenant Redington's killer. I had to get Bucko Doyle alone today and find out what he knew about the crime.

"Why did Doyle come to you?" I had asked Verity while we worked on my uniform. "Why not go to Lounsberry, or that Kellogg fellow?"

"I believe he thought I would be susceptible to his 'manly charms,' " Verity said with a raised eyebrow. "He probably thought he could get a two-for-one arrangement. I soon dissuaded him of that."

"You have a natural ability in that regard," I admitted.

Doyle told Verity that he'd sneaked out of the guard house the night of Redington's death, on his way to see a "friend," presumably Kitty Daugherty. Near Officers Row, he'd seen two men carrying something slung between them—at the time he'd thought it was a sack. One of the men talked, and Doyle recognized his voice as that of an officer at the fort. When he heard about Redington the next day, he realized what the men had been carrying.

"He's lowered his demand to a hundred and fifty dollars," Verity said. "He's scared. He wants to leave Fort Lincoln before something happens to him. There's nothing I can do, though. It's still more money than I can get hold of, based on what he's told me. I tried to explain that, but he doesn't understand. He has no proof, just the name of a man he thinks he recognized in the dark."

"The only proof we have is Redington's watch," I said, "and that was in Doyle's mattress."

"Maybe Doyle did kill Redington, and he's trying to pin the crime on someone else."

"I've thought about that."

I told Verity to leave the cottage that day and stay with the Lounsberrys. Stunned by what had happened to her dog, she agreed. "Keep away from Doyle," I added, "or anything concerning the Redington story till I get it cleared up."

Storm warnings rose in her green eyes. "Why—so you can have all the glory?"

"I'm not in this for glory. It's my job."

"It's my job, too. A few threats wouldn't stop my father or brother, and I'm as good as they are. I'll pursue this story wherever and whenever I can."

From the parade ground, "Reveille" sounded. Propping open my eyes, I went outside for roll call. There were no duties at the fort on Christmas and only a skeleton guard. Aside from morning formation, we had the day free.

"What happened to you this time, Hughes?" asked Sergeant Varden. The new cuts on my face went nicely with the layers of bruises and scrapes I had been accumulating. I looked like an archeological dig of pain.

"An accident, First Sergeant."

"You have more accidents than a Chinese railroad. Get that uniform squared away before you pull guard again, or I'll have you tied up by the thumbs. Come to think of it, why aren't you on guard today? I meant to fix the roster so that your name would come up."

I said nothing.

After breakfast we had a snowball fight with A Company. This Christmas battle was a tradition, "Wild I" against the "Forty Thieves," as A Company was called. It had started at Camp Supply in '68, and continued every year thereafter, circumstances permitting. The sergeants and corporals led us. There were volleys, charges, counter charges, flank attacks and strategic withdrawals. A few men were put out of commission with concussions and broken noses, and these were helped to the rear. Off to one side, the officers of both companies watched in a little knot, nodding among themselves and passing flasks of brandy.

At last a determined advance on our part routed the Thieves and left us in possession of the battlefield, the area between our barracks. We let forth a rousing cheer, while the defeated party groused and promised a better showing next year.

As the gathering broke up, I walked over to Bucko Doyle. In a low voice I said, "I need to—" but before I could finish, he hit me in the jaw, knocking me down.

I got up and charged him. I'd had it with this jug-eared son of a bitch. "I'll kill you!" I shouted. I barreled into him and we went down in the snow, punching and scratching.

Sergeant Morgan yanked us apart. "Get up, you fools, before Varden sees you. You want to be in the mill for Christmas?" He hauled us to our feet, tossing us in different directions, like we were potato sacks. Doyle glared at me and went back to the barracks.

"See you two ain't made up yet," Morgan said to me.

"Don't look like it's gonna happen anytime soon, either," I replied, breathing hard. I followed Doyle into the barracks, where I changed into my dress uniform, with its yellow collar and sleeve facings, and got ready for the jollification.

The men had begun preparing for Christmas months ago, using the company funds to place orders for canned foods and liquor at the trader's store. The officers had spent the last few days hunting along the river bottoms, and Captain Keogh and Lieutenant Porter had each donated a deer for our table, the men not being allowed to hunt for fear they would desert.

A crested punch bowl was set up in the middle of the barracks, and Whitey Tarr made a rum punch he'd learned years ago, as a dragoon. The barracks roared with laughter, horseplay, and impromptu dancing to the music of banjo, mouth organ, and penny whistle.

Two-Bit had taken over the kitchen for the day, displacing the regular cooks. He came back to change his uniform and get some punch. Dick Daring slicked down his blond hair, admiring himself in a small mirror hung from his shelf. He joined Two-Bit at the punch bowl. "I'm gonna miss you criminals this time next year," he announced, "when I'm in school learning how to be a gentleman."

"What about you, Sarge?" Two-Bit called to Morgan, who was buttoning his tunic. "You gonna miss us?"

"Fat chance," Morgan snorted. "I'm gonna have me a wife this time next year. I'll be too busy making babies to miss you screw-ups."

There was hooting and laughter, but I was only half paying attention. The sounds and smells had taken me back—to Christmases with the Danvilles, in Texas. In those days there wasn't a church within fifty miles, so Pa Danville, old Sixtus, read the Bible on Christmas morning and we sang hymns; while the dog-trot cabin filled with the smell of Ma Danville's turkey, with its sausage and cornbread stuffing, baking in the kitchen. There was always a small present for each of us children—a knife or flannel shirt for the other boys; a gingham dress for the girls; a book for me, ordered all the way from New Orleans. After we ate, Pa played the fiddle and there'd be more singing. Sometimes, when the weather was good, we drove to the nearest neighbors or they came to our place and there'd be dancing—me and Lydia, the other youngsters, their folks. Those had been happy times, but I had always been a bit sad underneath, knowing I really wasn't a Danville, wondering what Christmas would have been like with my own family.

Dick sat on the foot locker next to mine. "Thinking

about the old days?"

"Yeah."

"Christmas does that to you. The thing I remember best is how, each year on Christmas Eve, my dad would go out and scrounge us a pig to roast next day. It was the damnedest thing the way he did it. And he always bought Mom a new dress. And she always acted surprised, like she didn't know that was what she was going to get." He sighed. "It all changed after Dad got hurt on that construction project and couldn't work no more. Mom had to do odd jobs, took in just enough to keep us alive. If you wanted anything for Christmas after that, you had to steal it."

Two-Bit drank some punch and smacked his lips. "For us, Christmas was a big day of churchifying, then a feast at my Uncle Mordechai's house. We'd exchange presents and stay the night there, all us kids sleeping in the loft—talking, giggling and practical joking till it was full on to dawn."

"Well, ain't that sweet," sneered Doyle as he buckled his belt. "At my house, all Christmas meant was that Pa got drunk earlier in the day than usual. He'd pass out, and we didn't have to worry about him beating us. That was our present."

"Too bad Peaches caught guard today," Dick said, ignoring Doyle. "Wonder what Christmas was like where he lived?"

"How could anybody tell?" Two-Bit replied. "They all spoke Italian."

Whitey Tarr leaned against the wall by his equipment pegs, brushing something from his cheek. "What's wrong, Whitey?" said Earnest Blorm. "Homesick?"

"You kidding?" snarled Tarr. "I been in the army so

long, I can't even remember Christmas on the outside. Something in my eye, is all."

Two-Bit returned to the kitchen. A few minutes later he appeared at the door, dinging the mess triangle. "Dinner is served, gentlemen."

Everyone started for the mess hall. As they did, I pulled a pad from my coat and wrote in pencil: "Meet me behind the ice house after mess. Concerns Redington—Verity Winslow. Urgent. Hughes." I underlined "Urgent" twice, then folded the note, rose, and casually deposited the note on top of Doyle's folded mattress. I hoped to hell the bastard could read. As I turned away, I saw Whitey Tarr watching me. What the hell, it was too late now. I joined the last men filing into the mess hall. Tarr waited a second, then followed.

CHAPTER 24

Painted paper wreaths and balls adorned the mess hall walls and hung from the ceiling. When everyone was seated, Sergeant Varden stood at the head of the room. Tapping a tin mess cup with his knife, he raised his voice. "Men, before we start our Christmas celebration, let's take a moment to remember our comrades in I Company who have gone before us this year. I give you Patrick Shaughnessy, Otis Aldworth, and Hans Kleg."

We bowed our heads in silent prayer. Shaughnessy had died from an accident; Aldworth from fever. Hans had been well liked, and around the room there were threats of revenge against the Sioux, who had supposedly taken his life. Sergeant Morgan and I exchanged glances. We knew better. From the corner of my eye, I saw Whitey Tarr give a half smile.

Now the mood lightened and the feast began. We stuffed ourselves on Two-Bit's baked ham, fried oysters, venison with Madeira sauce, beef and kidney pie, biscuits with jelly, and canned cranberries. The meal was topped with a magnificent raisin duff, which Two-Bit flamed with brandy to a thunderous cheer.

"Two-Bit, you outdid yourself," said Dick Daring, unbuttoning his jacket and patting his stomach. "You should open a restaurant."

"Eat it now," Two-Bit said. "You know what we're having tomorrow."

"Beef, bread, and coffee," groaned a half-dozen men

in unison.

There was a commotion at the mess hall door, and Captain Keogh came in, followed by Gentleman Jim Porter. Keogh wore his dress uniform, with braided shoulder pads, aigullette cords, and tassels; a cigar was jammed in his mouth and his arms were filled with whiskey bottles. Under his plumed helmet, his face was already red. "Happy Christmas, men!" he cried.

We shouted a reply.

Porter carried another armload of bottles and a box of Cuban cigars. The whiskey was prime Maryland rye, not frontier rotgut. The bottles were opened, the cigars passed around. The musicians began playing again. We sang all the Christmas songs we knew, and from there went to bawdy versions of tunes like "The Girl I Left Behind Me." Finally, inevitably, we sang "Garry Owen," Keogh leading us, banging our cups on the tables in time with the words:

> "Instead of Spa we'll drink down ale.
> And pay the reck'ning on the nail;
> No man for debt shall go to jail
> From Garry Owen in glory."

From outside there came an echo. The other companies were singing "Garry Owen" as well, the tunes rising from the mess halls, mingling and floating across the parade ground into the waning winter afternoon. I joined in, roaring along with the rest. It was impossible not to get caught up in the spirit.

We were the Seventh Cavalry. We were invincible.

Keogh and Porter departed, to prepare for the grand affair at Custer's house, but our party went on. Men came and went—to use the latrines, play cards, or visit friends in other companies. Bucko Doyle left briefly, then returned. He glared at me when he walked in, but gave no hint that he'd seen my note. Maybe he couldn't read, I thought, or maybe Tarr had taken the note before Doyle had a chance to see it.

After a while, Doyle slipped out of the mess hall again. I waited a few minutes, and when he didn't come back, I followed. He wasn't in the barracks; his overcoat was gone from its peg. I got my coat, put on my dress helmet, and went after him.

As I came down from the porch, I ran into Lieutenant Granville, who must have been leaving A Company's party. I saluted, but Granville braced me. "Hughes—just the man I wanted to see."

Granville wore no overcoat, despite the cold, and in the growing darkness the Medal of Honor on his chest reflected the barracks light. "I went into Bismarck this morning, Hughes, to pay Miss Winslow the respects of the day. I was surprised to find her staying at the Lounsberrys'."

I said nothing.

Granville's voice rose, increment by increment. "It took some doing on my part, but she finally told me why she'd moved out of her cottage. She said she was attacked by two men last night. She said they shot pistols at her. She said she was forced to shoot one of them in self-defense."

"Really, sir? That's horrible."

"After a lot more prodding, she told me she wasn't alone in this little escapade. Guess who was with her?"

"Can't imagine, sir."

"It was you, Hughes!" Spittle flecked my face as he swore. "You son of a bitch, I told you to keep away from her."

"Yes, sir."

"Why didn't you?"

I said nothing, shifting my feet. I needed to get to the stables to meet Doyle.

Granville got control of himself. "She also—again, with a good deal of prodding—told me who you really are. That's the only reason I don't beat the stuffing out of you right here. I realize you're doing a job for General Custer."

"Yes, sir."

"That explains a lot about your recent actions. It does not explain why you risked Miss Winslow's life. Tell me, Hughes, have you ever been in love?"

"Yes."

"Would you have involved your lady in an affair like this?"

I hesitated. "No," I admitted.

"Then why did you involve mine!"

I had no answer. "You're right. I shouldn't have done it. I apologize."

"Apology not accepted. And why the devil were you two snooping around Amos Haselmere?"

Again I hesitated. "It was Haselmere's men who warned Verity—Miss Winslow—off the Redington story that night in Bismarck. It was Haselmere's men who attacked us yesterday."

Granville frowned. "Haselmere? You're sure?"

"I'm sure."

He rubbed his jaw. "But that doesn't make sense.

How could Haselmere be involved in this?"

"That's what I'd like to find out."

Granville straightened, his jaw set. "Let me find out. I'll make the bastard talk."

"No. I'll handle this. We don't need another dead officer."

"We don't need Verity dead, either, and that's what you almost got us."

"Verity's out of this now. The only one who's at risk is me. Let me do my job."

Granville looked unconvinced. "Very well," he said at last. "But you promise to leave Verity alone."

"I promise." Keeping Verity out of this was fine with me. Let somebody else deal with her.

"If I learn that you've involved her—even made contact with her—I will consider it an affair of honor. Do I make myself clear?"

"Quite clear." I didn't like being talked to this way, but I couldn't blame him. "Look, since you know who I am, can I ask you a few questions?" As much as I wanted to get to the stables, I might not get this chance to talk to Granville again. There was no guarantee Doyle was going to tell me anything, no guarantee he even knew anything. For all I knew, he might be running a confidence game with Verity.

Granville waited a long second. The two of us were alone. The sky had clouded with the prospect of more snow. Inside, the company parties were going full blast. Granville and I were inconspicuous in the dark, and even if we were seen, if there was one day an officer could talk to an enlisted man without drawing attention, it was today. Reluctantly, he said, "What do you want to know?"

"You were friends with Redington, weren't you?"

"I was as good a friend as he had, I suppose. I admired his energy, his intelligence. I thought he would prove to be brave, as well, though you can't be sure of that until a man's been tested under fire."

"A lot of the men—and some officers—hated him."

"He might have grown out of his problems with the men. Not everyone is a born leader, like General Custer. There's a learning process involved."

"And his problems with the officers?"

"I'm not defending—or excusing—Peter, but he didn't do anything a lot of other men haven't done. In wartime, his misdeeds might have gone unnoticed, but in peacetime, when people have nothing to do but gossip, things get magnified out of proportion. I pulled my share of damn fool stunts as a young man. I'm sure you pulled a few yourself."

I raised my brows. "Point taken."

"Peter wasn't a bad person. I think he would have made a decent officer in time. Whatever his faults, he didn't deserve to pay for them with his life."

"You've been with the regiment since it was formed, haven't you?"

"That's right."

"Do you know why Whitey Tarr transferred in?"

"He said it was for the bonus money, but from his service records I learned he'd been in a fight and killed a man."

"Any idea what the fight was about?"

"His records didn't say. Usual drunken row, I expect."

"But no charges were filed?"

"Apparently not, but I assume he felt uncomfortable

in the Second after that. Probably the C.O. made him transfer."

I digested this information. "You know that Redington had a fight with Lieutenant Manley the night of his death?"

"I was there when it happened."

"A bad fight?"

"As bad as I've seen among officers. The guards had the devil's own time breaking it up."

"I have a witness who claims that Manley threatened to finish the job. Any idea if he did?"

Granville thought back. "Well, he left the club immediately afterward, but I don't know where he went."

"Was he capable of killing Redington?"

"Who—King? I don't know. I mean, maybe if he was angry enough. I heard he shot another officer in a duel during the war, and he's certainly jealous of Evangeline. But I thought an enlisted man killed Peter?"

"There's some doubt about that."

In the darkness, I saw Granville's eyes narrow. "You suspect King Manley?"

"It's possible. You knew Redington had gambling debts?"

"To Eddie Erickson, yes. But Eddie didn't kill him. Peter settled up."

"Do you know where he got the money?"

"No. Thought it was strange when he came up with it, though."

"Could he have stolen it?"

"Who from? Who has that kind of money out here?"

"Did you ever see him with Amos Haselmere?"

"Finally we get back to Haselmere. I've only seen them together in the store."

"Not socially?"

"Haselmere does his socializing in town. The officers snub him, because of the way he abuses his prerogatives of selling goods to us. That's why it's hard to see him being involved in this. Everybody hates him."

"Redington was acting Quartermaster when you were on temporary assignment, wasn't he?"

"That's right."

"Was there anything untoward in the performance of his duty?"

"No. Peter did a good job, actually. Coming in like that, with no training. Like I said, he was smart."

"Could he have stolen the money to pay his debts then?"

"You know, I thought about that myself. I checked the discretionary funds—twice—but nothing was missing."

I nodded. "Thanks for your help, Lieutenant."

"You're welcome. I can't say I like you, Hughes, but I wish you good luck in finding Peter's killer." He pointed at me. "Remember what I said about Verity." He turned and walked away without waiting for me to reply. I wondered if he was going after Haselmere, anyway. I just hoped he didn't do anything stupid.

I ran to the ice house, hoping I wasn't too late to catch Doyle. The ice house was behind the granary, at the northwestern corner of the parade ground. I had picked it because no one was likely to come there at this time of year. I hoped Doyle hadn't taken a funk and left. More than likely, he'd never come at all. He'd probably gotten the note and ignored it. He was probably at "Keetty" Daugherty's right now, while I was running through the snow, making a fool of myself.

Behind the granary, I saw a set of tracks in the snow.

That would be Doyle's. Good.

Further on, another set of tracks joined the first. "Christ."

I rounded the corner of the ice house and stopped. A black form lay sprawled on the snow.

It was a man, face down. I turned him over.

It was Doyle. The front of his uniform was drenched with blood. Sticking in his chest was an army issue field knife. I didn't have to see the serial number to know that it was mine.

CHAPTER 25

I felt Doyle's pulse. He was dead.

No signs of a struggle. His killer had been someone he knew.

The knife was buried in his chest up to the hilt. I worked it up and down, then pulled it out, getting my hands covered with blood in the process. It was my knife, all right; even in the dark I could tell by the unusual angle at which a previous owner had carved his initials in the handle. I had been set up.

It began to snow. At Custer's house, the regimental band struck up their first notes. From the other side of the post came the raucous sounds of the celebrations at Suds Row and the teamsters' quarters.

Should I call the guard? They'd never believe I didn't do this. I needed to take my knife and get out of here. I would probably be a suspect anyway, at least I wouldn't be in the vicinity when Doyle's body was found. I had to get to Custer's house and tell him that Doyle was not Redington's —

"Halt! Who goes there? Stand, and be recognized!"

I turned. Three figures were approaching, two with leveled carbines. It was the guard.

"Stand, there. Don't move."

The speaker was Lieutenant Manley, the red sash across his chest identifying him as Officer of the Day. He must be making his grand rounds of the post. One of the guards was Peaches—our eyes met, and he gave me a queer look as if to ask what I was doing.

"Got here awful fast, didn't you, Lieutenant?" I said.

"Speak when you're spoken to," said Manley. "What's going on here?" He saw my bloody hands, and the knife in them. He motioned Peaches to look at the body.

Peaches knelt. "It is . . . it is Private Doyle," he said. "From I Company." He rose, his voice soft now, shocked. "He is dead."

A cold smile crossed Manley's normally sour face. "Take that weapon, and place this man under arrest. If he tries to run, or resists in any way, shoot him."

The two guards loaded their weapons, then moved alongside me. I gave the knife to Peaches. He passed it to Manley, who handled it gingerly, trying not to get blood on his overcoat. "We'll save this as evidence. It's yours, I suppose?"

"I didn't kill him," I said.

"Save the lies for your court martial."

"But I didn't. I just got here."

"Be quiet! Stella, Driscoll—take him to the guardhouse."

Peaches looked at Driscoll, a wiry southerner who prodded me with his carbine barrel. "Prisoner— atten-tion. Forward—march."

We skirted the parade ground on the barracks side, instead of taking the shorter way past Officers Row, to avoid offending the sensibilities of those attending Custer's ball. Across the parade ground, seen through the falling snow, lights blazed from Custer's huge house; the band was playing selections from Offenbach's *Gaite Parisienne*. Manley could scarcely conceal his elation at getting revenge for whatever slight he felt I'd done to him. Peaches kept glancing sideways at me. I knew he wanted to ask what had happened, but couldn't because of the officer's presence.

The guardhouse was a log structure with an anteroom for the guards and a larger holding area in the rear for prisoners. "Sergeant of the Guard!" called Manley as we approached.

The door opened, and a man looked out. The man's head was shaven and slightly pointed at the top, like a minie ball; he wore a moustache and goatee. It was Sergeant Finley of C Company. "This man is under arrest for murder," Manley said. "Lock him up."

Scrubbing his eyes—he must have been sleeping— Finley looked from Manley to me. Behind him, two more guards scrambled to their feet—all that were present because of the holiday. "Yes, sir," Finley said. He motioned me into the guardroom. "In here."

Manley turned to Peaches. "Send for your first sergeant. I'm going to the General's house, to notify Captain Keogh and Doctor Lord. Driscoll, guard the body until the doctor arrives. Sergeant Finley, put this knife in a secure location. It will be needed at the court martial."

Peaches started for the barracks; Driscoll headed back to the ice house. Manley turned and strode briskly away. I could picture his appearance at Custer's ball. Decorations, music playing, dancing. Heads turn as Manley enters, snow covering his caped shoulders, people wondering why the O.D. is here. He speaks to Keogh, then Lord. Keogh excuses himself and calls Custer away from his guests—or from his study, if that's where he is. Verity Winslow would be there, wondering what the fuss was about. Would she guess that I was involved? Knowing Verity, she might.

"Inside with you." Sergeant Finley shoved me through the door into the holding area. It was a large, low-ceilinged room with a stove and water bucket in the middle. It reeked of unwashed bodies and tobacco, of urine and feces where men had relieved themselves in the corners. There were no bunks, just the earthen floors to sleep on, with three cells in the back for more desperate prisoners. Right now the room was empty, the prisoners having been released to their companies to celebrate Christmas Day. Tomorrow they would be back again.

"What about my blankets?" I asked Finley.

"You can get 'em tomorrow."

"What am I supposed to do tonight?"

"Freeze, I guess. That ain't my problem."

"How about a match, so I can at least light the stove?"

Finley considered. "Hell, why not? It's Christmas." He tossed me a box of matches. "Who'd you kill?"

"Bucko Doyle, so they say."

Finley looked at me with new respect. He couldn't have been more than twenty-five or six. I heard he shaved his head because of a skin problem. "Figured somebody would kill Doyle one of these days."

"But I didn't—oh, the hell with it." He wasn't going to believe me anyway. I lit the stove and gave him back the matches.

As Finley shut the door and barred it, I spread my overcoat and sat on the earthen floor. It wouldn't be long before the floor's chill dampness began seeping through the wool coat. I tried to ignore the gut-churning stench and figure out what had happened.

Somebody had found my note, followed Doyle, and killed him. It was too much of a coincidence to have happened any other way. But who? Somebody who knew who I really was. Was there another way I could have handled the situation? Given the crowded conditions of a military post, and Doyle's personality, I didn't see one. If I could have talked to the stupid son of a bitch that morning, instead of fighting with him, I wouldn't have had to leave him the note.

One thing was certain—Doyle hadn't been running a shell game with Verity. He'd known something, and someone had been willing to kill him to keep him from telling. But Doyle had said Redington's killer was an officer. No officer could have read that note except Keogh or Lieutenant Porter, and it was hard to picture either of them as a murderer.

There were noises from the guard room. The bar was lifted, the door opened, and Captain Keogh entered, followed by Sergeants Varden and Morgan. I rose. Keogh looked at me thoughtfully, tapping his silver-headed cane in the palm of his gloved hand. Morgan handed me my blankets, neatly folded.

"Thanks," I said.

Varden blew on his hands to warm them, wrinkling his nose at the air in the fetid room. "I knew no good would come of you, Hughes. Still and all, not only are we rid of you, we've gotten rid of the company's biggest troublemaker in the bargain—though Doyle was a good man to have in a tight spot."

"I didn't kill him."

"Of course you did. Don't play innocent with me. The guards found you bending over the body with a bloody knife in your hand—who else could have done it? There's been bad feelings between you and Doyle ever since you joined up. Not only that, but Sergeant Morgan, here, heard you threaten to kill Doyle this very morning."

Morgan looked at me and spread his arms helplessly.

Varden went on. "In addition, Private Tarr has stated that before you went into dinner this afternoon, you left a note on Doyle's bunk. The note has disappeared, but I expect it told Doyle to meet you behind the ice house. I don't know what he thought was going to happen, but apparently you intended to settle scores.

"Don't look so worried, Hughes, I doubt they'll hang you—you didn't kill an officer, after all." (Keogh gave him a funny look for that remark.) "You'll likely get thirty years or so in Leavenworth. How old are you now—thirty-three? You'll only be sixty-three when you get out. Plenty of time to start a new life." He laughed.

Keogh pressed the cane against his imperial. He must have known I was telling the truth, but he didn't care. "You'll remain in the guard house until your court-martial convenes, Hughes. That could take several months. Tomorrow you go into one of the cells. You'll be allowed outside one half-hour each day, for exercise and to use the latrine. Any questions?"

"Plenty of questions, but I doubt I'll get any answers."

"That's all, then."

Varden and Morgan came to attention. Keogh waited. Varden prompted me. "Salute the officer, Hughes."

"What are you going to do if I don't—put me in the guard house?"

Keogh slashed at me with the cane. This time I was expecting it, and I grabbed it in mid-air. My eyes met Keogh's. "Once was enough, Capt—"

Varden punched me in the stomach, doubling me over. I let go of the cane, and Keogh whacked me across the back, driving me to one knee.

Keogh grinned. "It's a grand mouth you have,

Hughes. Someday it'll get you in trouble."

He turned to go. The others stood aside to let him pass. Finley and the two guards saluted; Keogh touched the cane to his helmet brim in reply. Varden followed him out the door.

Morgan hung back. He looked at me and shook his head. "I had no choice but to tell."

"I know. You believe me, don't you? I didn't kill Doyle."

"I'll take your word for it, but it looks bad. Anything I can do for you?"

"You can get me out of here."

"I wish I could. Good luck."

"Thanks."

He left. Sergeant Finley shut the door and barred it. I was alone in the empty room, the only light coming from the tiny pile of wood burning in the stove. The wood wouldn't last until morning, and I knew I wouldn't be able to get more.

I wrapped the blankets around me and huddled against the log wall. I closed my eyes, the distant music of the regimental band my lullaby.

I was dead tired and fell asleep immediately. It seemed I was no sooner out than I came awake again, swimming up from the depths of darkness.

What had alerted me? Noise from outside, a pounding at the guard room door. A flinty voice cried, "Doctor Lord, to see the prisoner."

Now what, I thought.

The guards let him inside. "Dragged out on Christmas night," he swore. "They want me to test this fellow, to see if he's crazy. Waste of time, you ask me. Well, don't just stand there, youngster — open the door, open the door."

The holding are door was unbarred, then opened, and Doctor Lord stepped inside. He stood looking around, stooped at the shoulders, wearing a long buffalo robe coat dusted with snow. All of his face but his eyes were hidden by a buffalo fur cap with enormous ear flaps, and a wool muffler that was wrapped around his mouth and nose.

"Leave us alone," he ordered Sergeant Finley.

Finley shrugged. "Whatever you say, Doc." He took a lantern from the guard room and hung it on a peg inside the holding area. Then he closed the holding room door and barred it.

With that, my visitor stood straighter, as if shedding his years. He removed the scarf and cap, revealing short, thinning hair and a set of jug ears. His piercing blue eyes twinkled.

I stood, shaking off sleep. "Hello, General."

CHAPTER 26

Custer chuckled gleefully and rubbed his hands together, like a schoolboy who has just pulled off a spectacular prank. "I fooled them. Ha ha, I did it. Wait till Libby and Tom hear about this. How did you find my portrayal of the good doctor?" He lapsed into his raspy New England accent. "Speak up, youngster, be honest." In his own voice he added, "My friend Mr. Lawrence Barrett would have been proud of me. I could have been an actor like him, you know. I'd have been a good one, too—no, a great one. Couldn't you see me as Tamurlane, or Henry the Fifth?"

He cast aside his buffalo-robe coat, revealing his dress uniform. He looked even more gaunt than usual. The lantern light played in the hollows of his face, accentuating his high cheek bones. He paced back and forth. "You've wrapped up this affair nicely, Hughes. Private Doyle is dead, so we've no need to put him on trial for Lieutenant Redington's murder. For general consumption, we'll continue to say that Redington died of natural causes. For the War Department, and the official record, we'll let it be known that the murderer was uncovered by a detective, who was forced to kill the suspect during his investigation. All nice and tidy."

"Except for two things," I said. "I didn't kill Doyle, and Doyle didn't kill Redington. Doyle knew who did it, though. The real killer silenced him and made it look like it was me."

Custer stopped pacing. His sunny mood dissipated. "Don't start this again."

"It's the truth."

"Do you have any idea who this 'real killer' is?"

"No."

"And your deadline for finding him was . . ?"

"Today."

"I'll tell you what I believe, Hughes. I believe that Doyle was the murderer, but you killed him for personal reasons. You admitted that you've killed men in cold blood before."

"That was different. Those men murdered my fiancée."

"Still, it bespeaks a certain vindictiveness on your part. I understand that you and Doyle fought on several occasions. Plus, he killed a man by mistake, didn't he? While you were on that patrol?"

"Hans Kleg."

"Maybe this Kleg was a friend of yours, and you wanted to pay Doyle back."

"Yes, I want to pay back the killer, but the killer wasn't Doyle! What do I have to do, draw you a picture? How the hell we lost the war with people like you running the other side is beyond me."

There was a noise outside. The guards had heard me yelling. "You all right, Doc?" Sergeant Finley called through the door.

Custer assumed the New England accent again. "If I'm in need of your assistance, Sergeant, I'll call for it." He looked at me, lips a thin line beneath the walrus moustache. "I'm not used to being spoken to that way, Hughes. I've a mind to horsewhip you."

"You know where to find me when you're ready to

try."

We faced each other for a moment, then I added, "That won't change the fact that the real killer is still at large."

Exasperated, Custer said, "You keep talking about the 'real killer,' but you never offer evidence that he exists."

"Really? Then why did Amos Haselmere's men try to kill me in Bismarck last night?"

"Haselmere? The post trader?"

"That's right."

"Are you saying that Amos Haselmere killed Peter Redington?"

"I'm saying that he knows something about it."

"That's the stupidest thing I ever heard." Custer took a turn around the room, twisting one end of his moustache. "I admit, it would make Libby happy—she can't stand Haselmere. Don't think much of him, myself, but I don't believe he's a murderer."

"Then why—?"

"I don't know! Frankly, I don't care. Every time I listen to you, it's something different. The killer is an officer, the killer is Haselmere, the killer is Father Christmas. Let's for the sake of argument say you're right, and Doyle wasn't the 'real killer.' How do you propose to find the man?"

"I don't follow you."

"There's no way I can let you out of the guardhouse— you've been arrested for another soldier's death. You'll be here about two months, until your court martial starts, and at least another month while it takes place, even if we rig the jury. Courts martial always take a long time, because of the paperwork. By the time you get out, the spring campaign will be under way, so the court martial might have to wait till we get back from fighting Sitting Bull—all of which time you'll be on my payroll. Let's be optimistic, say that the campaign gets delayed, and the court martial goes ahead on time. That's still a minimum of a hundred days at ten dollars a day—a thousand dollars. I don't have that much money, and if I did have it, I wouldn't give it to you for doing nothing. Because that's what you will be doing—nothing. You can't investigate while you're in the guardhouse. I can't release you back to I Company. You'd be compromised, not to mention in danger from the men. So, you see, your usefulness has ended. You've become an inconvenience."

"What do you propose?"

From his aiguilletted jacket, Custer drew an envelope. "Here's a hundred and fifty dollars, your pay for fifteen days' work. If you stay past midnight, I'll have to give you another ten. I had to borrow to get this much."

"You're letting me go?"

"Not exactly. I don't want the command to know you're a detective. We're going to let you 'desert.' There will be no pursuit—not much of one, anyway—and Lieutenant Cooke will quietly remove your name from the company rolls. It'll be like you never existed—which would certainly have been my preference."

"What about my personal possessions? I've got some money hidden in my foot locker."

Custer grinned. "We all lose things sometimes. Fortunes of war. I remember I lost part of my baggage to my West Point roommate, General Rosser, during the war. Being me, of course, I got the best of him—a few days later, I captured his entire headquarters and got a brand new uniform of his. I still have it, wear it to masquerade balls. A good joke, eh—me, going as a

Confederate general?"

"Well, I guess I'm not going to capture your headquarters, but when you go to auction my things, the boys are going to wonder where I got that much money."

"Hm, a good point. I'll tell Colonel Keogh to quietly confiscate the money when he inventories your effects. He can donate it to the company fund."

"And the killer?"

"Texas, you're beginning to bore me. The evidence -- which, I might add, you provided – proves that Private Doyle killed Lieutenant Redington. Doyle is now dead himself, and as far as I'm concerned, that's an end to it. The regiment can be at peace again. There is an Indian battle coming. I expect to be in it. I expect to win it. That victory is mine by right, and I will do nothing that may jeopardize my achieving it. You should be happy. I'm as good as my word – you found the killer, and I'm releasing you from your enlistment. I could see that you serve out your five years in the guardhouse, if not Leavenworth."

He tossed me the envelope. "It's a shame you killed Doyle and not an innocent man, because I would have enjoyed presiding at your court martial. Good day to you, sir."

He put on his "disguise," wrapping the muffler securely around the lower part of his face. He hunched his shoulders and rapped on the door. "Sergeant of the Guard!"

There was a scraping as the bar was drawn. Without a backward look, Custer departed.

I stuffed the envelope in my overcoat and sank back on the earthen floor, warming my hands at the stove. Through the ventilation grill, the reflection from the snowfall outside helped brighten the room, taking the edge off the shadows cast by the stove's weak fire.

There was a commotion from across the parade ground. Agitated voices. Another voice shouted from close at hand. "Guard—turn out!" It was Sergeant Morgan. "Turn out—there's a fire at the commissary!"

From the guard room came the sound of scrambling feet. The front door opened, and I heard Morgan say, "Lieutenant Manley sent me. Hurry up!"

Finley and the guards left the room. The ventilation grill faced the wrong way, so I couldn't see anything. A moment later, Morgan's voice came through the door. "Hughes?"

"Here!"

I heard the bar being drawn back. "Break it down," Morgan said. "It has to look like you did it."

I threw myself against the heavy pine door. "Hurry up!" Morgan said. I wasn't surprised they'd sent Morgan to spring me. I threw myself at the door again, was rewarded by the sound of splintering wood. Once more — this time there was a loud crack, and the door gave way. I kicked it open the rest of the way and stepped into the guard room.

"Come on," Morgan said. "I've got a horse waiting out back."

"Wait," I said. There were no weapons in the guard room; the guards had taken theirs with them. I opened the sergeant's desk, found my bloody field knife and slipped it into my coat. It was better than nothing if I ran into trouble.

I followed Morgan out the door. Across the parade ground, I saw the fire. It was a small blaze in one of the sheds behind the commissary, just enough to create a diversion. I saw men milling round, highlighted against the flames, smelled burning embers through the driving snow. "Custer told me they were going to let me desert."

"Desert?" Morgan barked a laugh. "You're not going to desert, they're planning to kill you."

My stomach went cold. For some reason, I wasn't surprised.

"I heard them talking about it," he went on. "Decided to beat them to it."

"You started the fire?"

"Yeah."

We ran behind the guard house, Morgan letting me take the lead. It was dark, the snow falling. "Where's the—?"

Something made me turn. I saw Morgan stepping forward, saw the blade coming toward me, the same way it must have come at Bucko Doyle. Desperately I twisted out of the way. Morgan twisted with me, and the knife blade caught the front of my coat, ripped it open, then snagged on the buttons.

I grabbed his hand, but he was strong and ripped free. He slashed at my face. I jumped backward, lost my balance, fell. I landed on my back in the snow, and Morgan leaped on me, lips drawn back in rage, teeth showing like a wild animal's. He stabbed at my chest; I shifted, and the blade went into my shoulder. As he pulled the knife free and raised it again, I caught his wrist. He put both hands on the handle and pressed as hard as he could, face straining. Down, down came the blade, overpowering my efforts to resist, until the point was touching my chest. With one hand I reached up, jammed my thumb in his eye, and twisted. He screamed and fell part way off me. I reached in my coat, found my knife, drew it out. As he came at me again, slashing, half blind

182

and maddened with rage, I stabbed him in the neck, severing his jugular vein.

He waved his arms spasmodically. Blood spurted from his neck and mouth. In slow motion he toppled over, dropping his knife, grasping for me as I scrambled out of his way. The blood formed a spreading stain on the snow beneath him.

I got to my hands and knees, gasping for breath and having a hard time getting it in the thin, cold air. Thoughts whirled through my mind. It was Morgan who had killed Doyle, Morgan who shot Hans Kleg on that patrol, Morgan who hid the watch in Doyle's mattress, Morgan who had followed me into town from the fort, Morgan who set Haselmere's shoulder hitters on Verity Winslow and me.

Morgan was the one who said Doyle had threatened to kill Redington. Nobody else had heard it. Morgan had made sure I knew it was an army carbine that shot Hans; Morgan "had to" tell Keogh that I'd sworn to kill Doyle this morning. Morgan had known who I was all along. While pretending to look out for me, he'd really been keeping an eye on me—and trying to kill me.

Had Morgan killed Redington? He must have been part of it, but why? Was he acting with Haselmere? Again—why? What could have brought those two together? Or was there someone else involved, a third man?

Snow stung my eyes. My shoulder felt like a hot poker had been stuck in it. It was bleeding like hell, but I didn't think anything vital was severed. I turned Morgan over and held up his head. The light in his eyes was dimming rapidly. "Who's in this with you?" I demanded. "Who are you working for?"

His eyes turned to mine. He tried to say something but could only gurgle, his mouth filled with blood. As I bent closer to listen, there was a rattle in his throat. He shuddered and went limp.

I stumbled to my feet. I lifted Morgan by the shoulders, which didn't help my own shoulder any, and dragged him deeper into the shadows. Someone would find him before long, and the fort would be alerted, but I wanted to delay the process as long as possible. There was a huge amount of blood on the ground, but I couldn't do anything about that. The snow would soon cover it.

Morgan's plan must have been to kill me, then dispose of my body. That way it would look like I'd "deserted," the way I was supposed to. When Keogh or Varden, or whoever Custer sent to break me out, got to the guard house, they'd find me already gone. They'd figure I skipped during the fire, and that would be the end of me as far as the Seventh Cavalry was concerned.

I left Morgan and crossed the parade ground, toward the fire. Ahead of me there were shouts, men running back and forth. The guards had formed an improvised bucket brigade. Other men were shoveling snow onto the blaze, which was almost out. Some of the men were already going back to their barracks parties. Finley and the other guards would be returning to the guard house in a few minutes—to find me gone.

I tilted my plumed helmet over my eyes and joined the men fighting the fire. I found Peaches on the bucket line, his carbine stacked with those of the other guards. I took a place beside him. When he handed me the next bucket, he did a double take and his eyes widened. "Pretty Boy! What are you—?"

"Sh-h-h! Keep your voice down."

He looked around. None of the men was paying us any attention in the confusion and darkness and falling snow. Besides, most of them were drunk. "How do you get out of the mill?" Peaches said. "What has happen to your shoulder?"

"It's a long story. Listen, now, and don't say anything. You've got to trust me. I just killed Sergeant Morgan."

His eyes opened even wider, if that was possible. "You have what!"

"Sh-h-h! Morgan killed Bucko Doyle. He was involved in Lieutenant's Redington's murder, too."

Behind Peaches, the next bucket came along. I rapped Peaches' shoulder. He remembered what he was supposed to be doing, turned and took the bucket. I took it from him and passed it to the next man down the line. "You've got to help me get out of here," I told Peaches.

"Me? How?"

"Go to the stables. Saddle Smoke and another horse — your own horse, Briar, would be good. Leave them at the wagon park, by the water tenders."

"But—the fire."

"It's almost out. Get the horses on your way back to your guard post. Bring my field uniform, too, if you can. Be quick."

"Why two horses?"

"I have to get someone."

CHAPTER 27

I learned early in life, if you want to find a woman, wait by the privy. They're bound to show up there sooner or later. In my experience, it's usually sooner.

Making my way through the falling snow, I took a place behind Custer's house with a view of the back door and latrine. Inside, the regimental band—who were nearly all Germans—was playing a polka. I watched the procession of women and men hurrying to and from the latrine, and prayed that Verity Winslow would be alone when she came.

She was.

She came down the shoveled walk, wearing a low cut green dress with a bustle and long frilly train, her red hair braided in ringlets down her back. Around her neck was an ivory cameo on a black velvet ribbon. I was a gentleman and waited till she was finished. As she came out of the latrine, I slipped up behind her and clamped a hand across her mouth.

Her response was a muffled scream. She kicked at my feet and ankles, threw herself from side to side, and bit my hand. "Ouch!" I yelped. "It's me—Lysander."

She looked over her shoulder, recognized me. I let her go, shaking my hand—she had a bite like a bull mastiff.

"I've been expecting you," she said, straightening herself and glancing around to make sure no one was coming. "I knew you were in some kind of trouble when King Manley showed up." Then she saw my wounded shoulder. "You're bleeding!"

"I'm always bleeding. We've got to—"

"And your hands—there's blood all over them. What—?"

"I'll tell you later. We have to get out of here."

"*We* have to? Why?"

"Your life's in danger." Still shaking my hand, I led her into the shadows, so we wouldn't be seen by others coming to use the latrine. "Doyle's dead."

She cupped her mouth. "Oh, my God. What happened?"

"A sergeant from my company named Morgan did it. He killed Doyle before I could learn anything from him. He made it look like I did it, then he tried to kill me too. He was part of the bunch that killed Redington. If these people want me dead, they probably feel the same about you."

From the direction of the guard house came shouting. "Hear that?" I said. "They're after me. I just broke out of the guard house."

Verity seemed resigned to leaving. "Are we going back to Bismarck?"

"No. That's the first place they'll look."

"Where then?"

"I don't know. But if we stay around here, we're going to be killed."

"It's freezing—can I get my coat?"

"No. Take mine." I slipped off my overcoat and draped it across her shoulders.

"But Reed—Lieutenant Granville. He'll think—"

"Send him a letter. Now, come on." I dragged her away, and she followed reluctantly.

Around the fort, there were shouts from the guards

looking for me. They'd head for the stables first. I hoped Peaches had beaten them there. To avoid being seen, Verity and I took the long way to the wagon park, sneaking behind Officers Row, the scouts' tipis, Suds Row, and the magazine. Though the snow was falling heavily, I smelled wisps of smoke from the charred remains of the commissary shed. The sounds of Christmas revelry were all around us.

There were no walkways shoveled where we were going, and Verity followed me as I punched a path through the snow. "I hope you're happy," she said, holding the train of her dress high. "These shoes are ruined. My feet are freezing."

"Extremely happy. I only did this to ruin your shoes."

Ahead was the wagon park. The rows of wagons made ghostly, rounded shapes in the falling snow. I heard a distant shouting for the sergeant of the guard. They must have found Morgan's body—I'd hoped it would take them longer. A whistle started blowing. As we neared the ungainly wooden tankers used for hauling water from the river, I squinted ahead. "There they are," I said with relief.

Two horses stood saddled and tied to the tanker wheels. The horses shook their heads and tugged at their halters, less than enthusiastic about having been dragged out of a warm stable. As we came up to them, Verity said, "How am I going to ride in these clothes?"

My field uniform was draped across Smoke's saddle. I shook the snow off it and tossed it to her. "Use these."

She looked at the blue jacket and trousers, looked at me. "You're kidding."

"Go ahead, put them on. I won't look."

"These pants must be five sizes too—"

"Use the galluses. Just hurry, will you? I don't want to be killed because your sense of fashion is offended."

I looked away. I heard rustling as she removed her dress with its bustle and long train. "They'll think you kidnapped me. Reed will follow you to the ends of the earth. He'll kill you."

"Reed's a soldier. His duty comes first. They're not going to let him go chasing us for personal reasons."

"The Seventh, then. They'll hunt us —"

"Don't flatter yourself. The only civilian the Seventh cares about is Libby Custer. Your fate doesn't concern them. They may come after me, but it'll be for killing Sergeant Morgan, not for —"

The rustling noise stopped. "You did what!"

"I told you he tried to kill me too. Now hurry up and get dressed."

A minute later she said, "I'm done."

I turned. Despite the urgency of the situation, it was hard not to laugh. A soldier Verity was not. Yet even wearing the baggy uniform, she managed to look prim and proper. Elegant, almost. She threw her dress and train over the front of her saddle. "I'm not leaving these here. It cost Reed too much to buy them." Then she shrugged into my overcoat.

I untied Peaches' horse Briar and helped Verity into the saddle. The horse stamped and curvetted at the feel of an unfamiliar rider, but Verity brought him under control. Excited voices were coming closer as I mounted Smoke.

"There he is!" came a shout.

"Christ," I said, "let's go!" With my helmet I smacked Briar's rear, yelling "Yah!" I dug my heels into Smoke's flanks.

Through the snow there was a flash and a bang. A

second carbine went off. I couldn't tell where the bullets went. We galloped out of the wagon park, headed west onto the prairie. Behind us a bugle blew "Boots and Saddles," as the Seventh Cavalry organized its pursuit.

CHAPTER 28

"They'll never catch us in this weather," Verity yelled above the howling wind.

"We won't be able to go very far, either," I cried back. "We have to find a place to lie up." I had tied her reins to my saddle's near-side pommel ring. If we got separated, we'd never get back together.

The storm had become a blizzard. Between the darkness and the snow, it was just about impossible to see anything. The wind drove the snow into our faces and the faces of our horses. We dropped our heads and turned away from it. Figuring the wind was out of the northwest, I tried to keep it on my right cheek, hoping that way we'd be heading west. The cold turned my hands and fingers stiff, making it hard to grip the horse's reins. I tried to protect them at least a little bit by putting the hem of my jacket over them, but it didn't work. They turned colder, then numb; then they began to burn, like somebody was holding a candle flame to them. My cheeks and ears burned as well. My legs and feet were like blocks of wood; it was hard to stay in the saddle. I hadn't had any sleep to speak of in four days, I was flushed and dizzy with fever, and I was getting steadily weaker with the loss of blood from my shoulder.

We came to an embankment, or rather we almost fell over it. It was only the balking of the horses that made us realize something was there. It was either the Heart River or a tributary, depending on how much we'd gotten turned off course. Hell, in this weather it could even be the Missouri. I motioned Verity to dismount. "Get down!" I shouted over the wind.

Awkwardly, I dismounted as well. Verity and I staggered and stumbled like we were drunk. We had to lean against our horses until the blood in our legs started flowing enough that we could walk. The snow came halfway to our knees. It went down my shoes, turning my feet first wet, then even colder than they had been before. I couldn't imagine what it must be doing to Verity's feet with those thin evening shoes. I looked around, saw nothing but white. I was thirsty, tired. Oh, so tired.

Verity shook my shoulder. "Are you all right?"

I had almost fallen asleep. I snapped my head alert and nodded. Verity was shivering violently, and I knew we'd both be lucky not to freeze to death. "We've got to find a place to wait out this storm," I yelled.

We started over the lip of the embankment. The horses were reluctant to follow, especially Verity's mount, Briar, and we had to tug them. We were forced to feel our way in the snowy darkness. Verity and I both fell more than once. After a few false starts, we found a way off the rim. Once below the rim, the shrieking wind lessened to the point that you could hear yourself think. The top part of the bluff or embankment we were on—it was impossible to tell how high up we were—seemed to be made of sheer rock. We were in a natural cutway to the bottom. Blundering around, I found a crevice just big enough for Verity and me to wedge into. A small overhang would provide a bit of shelter from the snow. It was as good as we were going to get. Reeling, unsteady on my feet, I motioned Verity into the crevice. Nearby I discovered a gnarled, stunted cedar. I tethered the unhappy horses to it with the picket line. I unsaddled them, got the horse blankets, and huddled in the crevice alongside Verity.

My shoulder was still leaking blood from the knife wound; the drying blood formed a dark crust on my snow-covered jacket. The shoulder hurt like hell. "I need to look at that wound," Verity shouted in my ear.

I nodded weakly, and in the darkness she peeled off my uniform jacket. "Ow!" I yelled as she ripped the half-frozen cloth from the wound.

"Sorry. Do you have a knife?"

"In your coat."

She found the knife in the overcoat pocket. She tore off my linen collar, then cut away my bloody white shirt and the wool undershirt beneath it. Her frozen fingers worked slowly, clumsily. She dropped the knife once, groped for it in the dark and started working again. When the undershirt was cut away, she peered closely at the wound, then probed it with her fingers.

"Ow!" I yelled again, yanked from the edge of sleep by the pain.

"The wound's deep," Verity said. "I wish we had a fire. I could heat the knife and cauterize it."

"You'd probably enjoy that."

"You're darn right I would. I was nice and warm in Custer's house, I was having a good time. Then you drag me out here. I'd rather be murdered than freeze to death."

She took a handful of snow, packed it, and began scrubbing my wound with it. The snow's cold turned my shoulder blessedly numb. When the snow was dark with blood, she threw it away and got some more. Her face was inches from mine, peering intently at the wound, the elaborately braided ringlets of hair hanging down one side of her neck.

When the wound was clean, she probed it again. "I can feel bits of cloth in here." She picked them out as best she could, but it was dark and she was exhausted, and her fingers were so frozen, she could only get the biggest ones. "I'd like to have a needle and thread to sew this, but I couldn't use them very well right now. Of course I couldn't do any worse than the fellow that sewed your face."

"He had an excuse. He was drunk."

She unbuttoned my field jacket that she was wearing, pulled the white shirt beneath it out of her trousers. With the knife, she cut the shirt's hem into strips, and bound the strips around my wound.

"Shouldn't you cut your dress for this?" I asked weakly. "That's the way they do it in the dime novels."

"If you think I'm cutting up my best dress for you, Lysander Hughes, you'd better think again. It's probably ruined anyway from the snow, but there's always a chance I can save it. Assuming I live through this, which is unlikely."

"You mean, if you didn't have that shirt, you'd let me bleed to death?"

"You'll never know, will you?"

She had a hell of a time knotting the improvised bandage, but when she was finished, she pulled my shirt and jacket back over my shoulders. She took some snow and tried to moisten my lips, but she was shivering so badly that all she could do was splatter snow over the lower part of my face. I got more in my nose than in my mouth. The overhang didn't protect us completely, and snow was falling on my bare chest.

I was nodding in and out of sleep, feverish, teeth

chattering. I hoped the sleep didn't turn into something more permanent. Verity's condition was nearly as bad. She was so cold, she was crying. She rubbed my fingertips, blew on them, then stuck my hands in her arm pits to warm them. But I was too far gone. We both were.

Verity let out a long breath. She took off my jacket, stripped away the rest of my bloody shirt and undershirt. Then she pulled her white shirt over her head. She pushed me down and lay on top of me.

"I can't believe I'm doing this," she muttered.

She pulled the field jacket back over her, then the overcoat and the horse blankets. She pressed herself to me. I felt her bare flesh against mine, felt her body heat infusing me as she wrapped her arms around me. I was aware of her firm breasts and nipples against my chest. Her thick hair smelled of violets. My last thought was that Lydia's hair had smelled the same way.

The snow came down.

CHAPTER 29

I awoke with a start. My first thought was, am I still alive? I decided that I must be. I couldn't be this cold and be dead—not unless I'd been drastically misinformed about conditions in hell.

I saw darkness, smelled the wool of my overcoat, which had been pulled over my head, mixed with the violet scent of Verity Winslow's hair, which nestled against my chin. With my good arm, I pushed the coat away from my face. A heavy layer of snow fell off. We had been buried in a drift. Its insulation had protected us from the deadliest effects of the cold. Overhead, the sky was bright with sunshine, though we were in the shadows here below the rim of the embankment. It was still cold; that much seemed like it would never change. Wedged into the rocky crevice, with Verity on top of me, my back felt like it had been through some kind of Oriental torture.

Awakened by my exertions, Verity stirred.

"Alive?" I asked her.

"I'll let you know," she mumbled. She shifted slightly, and I felt her breasts move against my chest. The furnace-like warmth of her bare flesh radiated through my upper body. Her long flanks pressed against my thighs.

We lay that way a moment, like lovers, comfortable and unwilling to move. My teeth had stopped chattering; I was still feverish but not as bad as I had been last night.

Verity's head rested on the unwounded side of my chest, and I stroked her hair. "You saved my life," I told her.

"Mm." She sounded more embarrassed about what she'd done than anything else. "That wasn't exactly the way I expected to spend Christmas night." Then she said, "We can't stay like this forever. Close your eyes."

I did.

She eased herself off my chest. I felt cold air rush into the space between us, though we were still covered by my overcoat and the horse blankets. With the moves of a contortionist, she put on her clothes. I heard rustling, felt her moving against me. I smelled the sweet woman smell of her.

"All right," she said.

I opened my eyes. She was dressed once more in my field uniform, looking at me as if searching for something in my face, ringlets of red hair cascading on either side of her. She placed a finger on my face. Slowly, she ran it along the length of my scar. Then, in a business-like tone, she said, "Let's take a look at that shoulder."

She removed the bandage. I only yelled a little bit. "The bleeding's stopped," she said. Cutting more strips from the hem of her white shirt, she made a fresh bandage and tied it on. "This new scar should fit in well with all your other ones. Tell me, do you rent yourself out for target practice?"

"Only when I need money."

Then she stopped, and she fingered the heart-shaped locket that hung from my neck. "What's this?"

I said nothing.

"Can I look?"

"Why not?" I'd never let anyone look at the locket before, but it didn't seem to matter now.

Her long nails pried open the locket's brass clasp. I knew what she saw; I'd gazed at it a thousand times — two small, faded tintypes, grainy and pitted. One showed a thoughtful, dark-haired young man with a cravat tied in a large bow; the other, a beautiful, composed young woman in gingham, her blonde hair pulled back in a bun.

"My parents," I said.

Prodded by Verity's green eyes, I went on. "Most of what I know about them I learned from our neighbors and old letters. My father was a university graduate — I guess that's where I get my taste for reading. My mother came from a prominent family in Virginia. She left everything to marry him and follow him to Texas, back in the days of the Republic. He was an idealist, believed in the Texas cause. He died before I was born."

"What happened to him?"

"He joined the Mier Expedition. You probably never heard of it."

"As a matter of fact, I have. An invasion of Mexico. In '41?"

" '42. My mother was pregnant when my father left, though neither of them knew it. Dad thought it was his duty to go. It never occurred to him he wouldn't come back. The expedition was a disaster. The men that didn't get shot got captured, and Santa Anna decided that one in ten should be executed. They drew beans to see who died, a black bean meaning you faced the firing squad. My father drew black.

"So, Mother was pregnant, with two other children to raise and a farm to run, miles from anywhere. She could have gone back to Virginia, but she stuck it out. She was a strong woman. She was . . . she was killed in a Comanche raid when I was two, along with my older brother,

Ezekial."

"I'm sorry," said Verity in a low voice. Then she frowned. "I thought you said there were two other children."

"There were. My sister Becky was three. Her body was never found, so she must have been kidnapped by the Indians. I was discovered the next day, hidden in a clump of brush. I have no idea how I got there. This locket was around my neck. The locket belonged to Becky."

"How did you get it?"

"I don't know."

"And Becky, was she ever found?"

"No. From time to time there were reports of a white girl traveling with the Comanches — or so I was told later. I was too little to know much about it at the time. When I was old enough, I began looking for her. I've been looking for her ever since, whenever I get money to finance a trip. I've been all over Texas, the Nations, New Mexico. Even down into old Mexico — she could have been sold as a slave there. Sometimes there's been leads, or what I thought were leads, but I never found her."

I brushed something from my eye. "She'd be thirty-four now, if she's still alive. Mackenzie's brought the last of the Comanches in, but she isn't at any of the agencies."

"Do you think she's alive?"

"I don't know. I'll keep looking for her, though. If she's out there, I'll find her."

Below us, one of the horses whickered plaintively. "Better get going," I said. "We stay here much longer, we'll need a homesteading permit."

Stiffly, working the cold from our muscles as we knocked the snow off of us, we rose. From above the rim of the bluff the wind blew snow down on us in intermittent, swirling showers. I was burning with thirst, and I stuck a handful of snow in my mouth and sucked on it. "I'd give anything for some coffee."

"A little food wouldn't hurt, either," said Verity. Verity shrugged into my overcoat. I put on my helmet and what was left of my shirt, undershirt, and dress jacket. They weren't much protection against the cold. It would be even worse up top, exposed to the wind.

We gathered the horse blankets and saddles. About two steps out of the crevice, we halted, ignoring the drifting snow that blew down on our heads. Below us were the horses, tethered to the stunted cedar. Several yards below them was a sheer drop of at least thirty feet. A few steps further last night, and we would have plunged over it.

"No wonder the horses were unhappy," Verity said.

"Wish we had some grain for them. They'll find no grazing in this weather, that's certain."

While we saddled the horses, I told Verity about my fight with Morgan. I told her how Morgan had framed Bucko Doyle and killed Hans Kleg, and about Custer's visit to me in the guard house.

"Did Morgan kill Redington?" she asked.

"Not on his own. There was someone else behind it."

"Haselmere?"

"Maybe," I said, drawing my girth strap tight. "There's only one way to find out."

"What do you mean?"

"I'm going back to the fort. The answer's in Haselmere's store."

"Are you insane? The whole Seventh Cavalry is looking for you, and they're likely to shoot you on sight."

"The fort is the last place they'll look. If I can dodge

the patrols they sent after us, I should be all right."

"Be serious. You're going to wander in there under the eyes of two hundred and fifty men, and no one's going to see you? Not even you believe that."

"No, but it helps to sound optimistic."

She grabbed my arm. "Please, Lysander—Mister Hughes. Don't go back there."

"Worried about me?" I grinned. "Admit it—you like me."

"No. No, I don't, but that doesn't mean I want you to die. Forget who killed Peter Redington. Get away, while you still can."

"I can't do that. I signed on to do a job, and I have to see it through. That's what a professional does, Miss Winslow. It's a matter of honor."

"Is your honor worth your life? Does it matter that much?"

"It does to me. I have no family, no property. Without honor, I'm nothing. I said I'd find Lieutenant Redington's killer, and I'm going to do it, whether Custer wants me to, or not." I grinned at her again. "Besides, your life's in danger while the killer's on the loose. You could always say I'm doing this for you."

She rolled her eyes.

"I'll take you downriver to Fort Rice, first. I'll present you to Lieutenant Calhoun there, tell him what's happened. You'll be safe with him till this is cleared up."

"Oh, no. I'm coming with you."

I started to say something, but she beat me to it. "You can't stop me, so don't try."

It was useless to argue. "It'll be dangerous."

"Being anywhere with you is dangerous." She waved a hand around us. "How much worse can it get?

We led the horses up the slippery, drift-filled cut. Wearing the thin dancing shoes, Verity would be lucky if she didn't lose her feet to frostbite in the snow and bitter cold, but she didn't complain. She acted like the cold didn't bother her.

"Reed Granville asked me to marry him," she said.

I stopped and looked back at her. Her eyes met mine frankly. "What did you tell him?"

"You kidnapped me before I had a chance to tell him much of anything. What do you think I should do?"

"Do you love him?"

"Yes. I guess. I mean, I'm pretty sure. I haven't been in love before, so this is all new to me."

"You'll have to give up journalism, you know, and follow Granville from post to post. You'll be enlisting in the Seventh Cavalry, and Libby Custer will be your commanding officer."

Verity let out her breath. "I know."

"A lieutenant's pay isn't much. Does Granville have money?"

"No. His father was some kind of big financial speculator, but he went broke and lost everything. In fact, Reed told me he sends his parents money."

"And none of that scares you off?"

"Surprisingly—no. I never thought I'd consider giving up my career, but I guess that's what love does to you. All I know is, I don't want to give Reed up. I just hope he doesn't give me up—now that I've been dragged off by you. Reed's jealous of you, you know. Men never cease to amaze me. How could he be jealous of a man whose face looks like a road map?"

"Don't forget—I'm rude and ill-mannered, too."

"Exactly."

Suddenly Verity's horse Briar twitched his ears, and his head turned. At the same time, my horse Smoke stiffened.

"Sh-h-h!" I told Verity. I pinched Smoke's nostrils and motioned Verity to do the same with Briar.

She said, "What—?"

I put a finger to my lips.

The horses fought us a bit, then gave in. Their ears flicked, their heads bobbed. Their eyes were big.

After several minutes I heard a noise from the rim above us—a shuffling, crunching sound, coming closer. I looked behind me, and my heart stopped.

With my head, I motioned to Verity. She followed my gaze and stifled a gasp of terror.

The far rim of the bluffs ran higher than the one on this side. Along the rim wall, cast by the morning sun, was a line of moving shadows—riders, in single file, carrying rifles and lances.

I suddenly forgot how cold I was. I was sweating with fear, my heart thumping in my chest like a steam engine. I thought of the knife in Verity's coat. It wouldn't be much use, but it was the only weapon we had, and I'd do the best I could with it. I looked at Verity. With most women, I'd have worried about them screaming, or losing their heads and trying to run away, but Verity wasn't like that. She stood still, looking cool and composed, though she must have been scared out of her wits.

Fortunately the Indians were upwind of us. If they hadn't been, their horses would have smelled us—hell, the Indians would have smelled us themselves. I could certainly smell them. There were about twenty of them, all men—or so it appeared from the shadows on the rock wall—heading west, to join Sitting Bull at his great camp in the Powder River country. These were the men Custer would fight in the spring. Present danger aside, I was sorry for the poor devils, whose only future seemed to involve starvation or being mowed down by the carbines of the Seventh Cavalry.

At last the shadows disappeared. We waited a long time before we released the horses' nostrils. The cold seeped through me once more. I was never so happy to be frozen. Verity's composure finally gave way. Her face was drawn and pale. "What would have happened if they had seen us?" she said.

"They'd have killed me—" I didn't bother to tell her how slowly—"and taken you prisoner." Something about that idea made me laugh. "I can just picture you a prisoner of the Sioux. Serve 'em right. Come on, let's get going. It's not getting any warmer out here."

CHAPTER 30

Verity and I watched from the shadows as the guard paced by the commissary and quartermaster's store, on the north side of the parade ground. It was about three hours till dawn, freezing as always, with the ever-present northwest wind slicing through us. We hadn't seen any patrols on our way back. Either the weather was too bad, or Custer, true to his promise, had called off the hunt for us. We'd left our horses west of the fort and come the rest of the way on foot, using the gullies and ravines to avoid being seen by the guards. Verity had cut strips from my overcoat and wrapped them around her feet. It made for awkward walking, but helped keep her from losing the feet to frostbite. I was near the end of my endurance, because of the cold and my lack of heavy clothing. The only part of me that wasn't frozen was my wounded shoulder, and the least movement sent waves of pain through that.

The guard went past us, his footsteps crunching the snow as he turned the corner of the quartermaster's store. I motioned Verity forward. Bent double, still keeping to the shadows, we made our way to Haselmere's store. Fort Lincoln was dark save for lights from the guardhouse and post headquarters, where the Officer of the Day stayed. The only people awake at this hour were the duty guards—and probably not all of them.

I picked the locks on Haselmere's door and we went in. The drafty, unheated building felt like a Turkish bath after days of being outside in the cold. In the reflected light from the snow outside, I searched the store shelves until I found a box of matches and a lamp. "Would it be stealing if I took a pair of shoes and some stockings?" Verity asked, examining Haselmere's stock of civilian goods.

"I think we could overlook it this once, especially since Haselmere tried to have us killed. Steal me a coat while you're at it."

We went into the office, and I sat next to the safe. It was a Stripler safe—massive, reassuring, and easy to open. I held my ear to the dial as I turned it.

"Who taught you to do that?" Verity joked as she pulled the wool stockings over her numbed, swollen feet. "Jesse James?"

"Nah, Jesse gets the bank people to do it for him."

Verity's jaw fell. "You know Jesse James?"

"Sure, I know Jesse," I said, twirling the dial in the opposite direction. "Wouldn't call him a friend, though. It's certain I'd never turn my back on him. Frank James now, he's salt of the earth. A regular fellow. We rode with Quantrill together."

"Quantrill!" Verity exclaimed. Then she recovered and lowered her voice, jamming her feet into the shoes. "Quantrill? The murderer?"

"I'll tell you about it some time. Right now—" I listened as the last tumbler fell into place—"we have other things to do."

I tugged down the safe's handle and pulled open the heavy door. The inside of the safe was divided into two compartments, jammed with boxes and bags and legal documents bound with red ribbons. I struck a match and lit the lamp, trimming the wick as much as I could, so that there was barely light to read by. "You take the top," I told Verity. "I'll take the bottom."

"What are we looking for?"

"The account books."

We pulled things out, tossing them aside in our haste. Haselmere would know his safe had been broken into, but who cared? There was plenty of money—sacks of coins, wrapped piles of greenbacks—but we weren't interested in that, though I caught Verity watching from the corner of her eye to see if I'd steal some.

"Here we go," I said. I pulled out a heavy ledger, bound in green cloth. I opened it and picked a month when Redington had been at the fort—September. I'm no accountant, and it took me a while both to decipher Haselmere's large, awkward hand and to figure out how the books worked. "Let's see, in September, Haselmere purchased fifty-two head of cattle from Sioux City

Cattle—"

"Which we know doesn't exist," said Verity, who was still poking around the safe.

" —at seventeen dollars a head. The draft was made out to 'T. Richardson'—probably a fictitious name that can't be traced. He resold the cattle to the army at nineteen a head. That's a profit of a hundred and four dollars before expenses. Not bad, but not what I was hoping to . . . "

"Here, what's this?" Verity said. From deep in the safe she wrestled forth a large bundle wrapped in oilcloth. It was another ledger, this one leather with a brass clasp. "It's locked," she said.

"Not for long. Give me my knife." She handed me the knife from my overcoat. I wedged it under the clasp and with a vigorous movement snapped the lock.

"Mister Haselmere won't like that," Verity tisked.

I flipped through the ledger while Verity peered over my shoulder. There was still a faint scent of violets from her hair. The smell took me back to the night we'd spent in the crevice, and it was hard to keep my mind on the business at hand. This ledger covered the same dates as the first one, but the entries were different, more detailed. "These are the real books," I realized. "The others are false ones, for the government auditors."

I found September of this year. "This is interesting. 'Beeves—received, 52 head.' But this time there's no price listed."

"No price?" Verity said. "You mean—?"

"It looks like he didn't pay for them."

"You mean someone just gave him fifty-two head of cattle?"

"Apparently. But he still sold them to Uncle Sam at nineteen dollars a head. That makes his new profit . . . "

I started to work it out, but Verity beat me to it. "Nine hundred and eighty-eight dollars for the month — quite a difference."

"And that's just for meat. Here, look at all the other things he got—flour, ten tons; vinegar, a hundred and twenty gallons; salt, eight barrels; candles; coffee; sugar. All from Missouri Valley Grains. And all for free. About half, it looks like he flogged off to the army; the rest, to the local civilians."

"No wonder he can undercut the prices in Bismarck," Verity said. "He doesn't pay for his stock. Either he's tapped into one heck of a philanthropist, or he's stealing. But where can he be getting it from?"

I remembered the empty sack I had found in Haselmere's warehouse. "There's only one organization that handles goods in those quantities—the Indian agencies. These supplies were meant for the Indians. They were diverted to Haselmere."

"All that? My God, did they leave anything for the Indians?"

"Not much, is my guess. No wonder the Indians are starving. The agents fake the ration rolls to show that everything has been distributed. It's not in their interest to tell the army that the young men are running away. Somebody might ask why, and the swindle could be discovered."

Verity was still pouring over the ledger. "Look here."

She pointed to a bottom right-hand entry, marked "disbursements."

> "$500 . . . . . Mrs. Belknap
> $500 . . . . . O. Grant
> $350 . . . . . Schofield
> $350 . . . . . 'Q'
> $300 . . . . . 'R'"

"A list of payments," she said.

"Schofield, you remember him—the Indian agent at Standing Rock. 'O. Grant'—that must be Orvil, the president's brother. And Mrs. Belknap—that's the war secretary's wife."

"This scheme must go right to the top, if the War Secretary's in on it."

"He's probably behind it," I said. "Him and Grant. And this is just their take from one post trader. Think how many others must be operating the same way."

"Just the same, two thousand a month in payoffs kind of eats up Haselmere's profits, doesn't it?"

"I guess it's tough being a crook these days. Don't cry for Haselmere, though. He's doing all right, when you look at all the other things he's selling. And remember, he's got a monopoly on the sale of goods to personnel stationed at the fort." I glanced through the ledger. "It looks like the payoffs to Grant and Mrs. Belknap are the same every month. The other three change, depending on the profits. No wonder men pay a thousand dollars for these post trader licenses. They're really licenses to steal — from the army and from the Indians. It's a good scheme. The cattle are fattened on government grain at the agency, then St. Jacques and Whitehead bring them to Bismarck to be slaughtered. The dry goods are freighted here, then re-packed in Haselmere's warehouse, so no one can tell their origin, and delivered to the commissary or sold over the counter at the trader's store."

Verity went back and tapped the ledger entry for September. "Who is 'Q'"?

I let out my breath. "Haselmere must have a connection here at the fort. He couldn't be selling such a large quantity of stolen government goods to the army without somebody getting wind of it. Think about it — who would be most likely to find out?"

"Probably the officer who buys supplies for the . . . " Verity's voice tailed off, " . . . for the army. The quartermaster."

I nodded. "Reed Granville."

"Very clever," said a voice, "unfortunately for you."

CHAPTER 31

Verity gasped, as Granville stepped into the room, followed by Amos Haselmere. Granville wore civilian clothes and there was a sawed-off ten-gauge in his hands. Haselmere, oily as ever, carried the Smith & Wesson pistol.

"Don't learn, do you, Hughes?" said Haselmere. "You keep lighting lamps in the dark."

"Helps me see," I told him.

Granville's rugged jaw was set tight; his ice blue eyes betrayed no emotion. He'd be a dangerous adversary as a soldier, more dangerous than the excitable Custer. "We've been waiting for you, Hughes. Sitting over in Amos's house. I'll give you credit—you kept that light low enough, it wouldn't have been seen if we weren't looking for it. I knew you'd be back, if you didn't get killed in the blizzard. You're the kind that doesn't know when to give up and go away." He took in my torn jacket, crusted with dried blood. "You look like hell, by the way."

Verity's face had gone chalk white. She had that look of amazement on her face that people get when they've been shot. "Reed, I don't believe it. I can't believe it. Please say it's not true."

Granville turned to her. "I told you to stay away from him, Verity. Why couldn't you have listened for once?"

"Then it was you who killed Peter Redington?"

"Yes."

"But why?"

"Let me guess," I cut in. "When Redington was acting quartermaster, he went through your books. Somehow or other, he figured out what was going on and blackmailed you."

"Right again," Granville said. "He should have turned us in, but he thought our scheme was a good one, and he wanted in on it. Besides, he was desperate for money to pay off his gambling debts. He called it being our partner, by the way, said it sounded classier than blackmail. Amos and I weren't crazy about the idea, but it was better than being reported to the authorities, and there was plenty of money to go around, so we cut him in."

Verity said, "So the 'R' in the ledger is for Redington?"

"That's right. Things were all right for a few months. Then Peter became greedy. He wanted more—a lot more. More than we were making. We weren't prepared to give him that, so . . . "

"So you killed him."

Granville shrugged. "At first we were going to make it look like an accident—a rifle misfiring or something—but that didn't seem right. Then we thought having him disappear, or killing him in town, making it look like a street robbery. But either of those courses might have led to an investigation—military, civilian, or both—and we didn't want that. We were going to blame it on that pathetic cuckold Manley—we knew the army'd try to hush it up that way, to avoid a scandal—but then I had the even better idea of pinning it on Bucko Doyle. We would buck and gag Redington, just like Redington had done to Doyle. Manley's an officer, his family might ask questions. Nobody would care what happened to Doyle. He was a hard case, it was easy to believe he'd kill an officer. The only surprise was that he hadn't done it before."

"How did you get Sergeant Morgan to help you?" I asked him.

"Money. When all else fails, that usually does the trick. Morgan was my platoon sergeant when I was in I Company—I saved his life at the Washita. I appealed to comradeship, I appealed to loyalty, but he wanted no part in helping us kill Redington. I knew he was planning to get married when he got out. The poor bastard couldn't have saved more than twenty dollars in nine years in the service, so I offered him the money to purchase a nice-sized farm. He still didn't want to do it, but he couldn't pass up an opportunity like that. He owed it to his fiancée. Blaming the crime on Doyle didn't hurt, either — Morgan would be getting rid of one of his biggest military headaches that way. Then he accidentally killed that potato head—what was his name?"

"Kleg."

"That's right, Kleg. He was all broken up about that. Came to me in tears and said he wanted out. I told him he was in too deep. We all were."

"When you met me after the Christmas party, that was no accident, was it? You were waiting for me. You wanted to give Morgan time to kill Doyle. That's why you were willing to talk."

Granville smiled, pleased with himself.

Verity said, "So what's going to happen now?"

"I think you know the answer to that. There's no other choice, Verity. Believe me, in your case I wish there were."

Through all of this, Haselmere had been sitting on the edge of his desk, grinning at me. Now he said, "Not so smart now, are you, Hughes? What, no witty remarks? Here's one—instead of Lysander with an 'L,' you can be Corpse with a 'C.'"

I wasn't impressed. "If you fire that scattergun in here it's going to make a lot of noise. You'll be up to your ears in guards. You might be able to explain away killing me, the notorious deserter, but what are you going to tell them about Verity?"

Haselmere smirked. "I guess we'll just have to take you two somewhere else and do the job, won't we?"

"But first," added Granville, "it's way past time to shut you up."

He bared his teeth in a ferocious mockery of a grin. He swung the shotgun, and I saw the butt coming at me. It seemed to be coming in slow motion, yet I was powerless to get out of the way. Then my head exploded in bright lights and pain.

I was lying on my back. Warm liquid was running over my face. Someone bent over me. As my mind slipped beneath the waves of consciousness, I heard Haselmere say, "Christ, he's dead."

CHAPTER 32

The jolting brought me to.

I was in the rear of a buckboard, banging back and forth in what seemed to be a rutted path. There was a tarp over me. I smelled the old wood and chipped paint of the buckboard, along with the moldy oilcloth canvas of the tarp. My face was caked with dried blood; it filled my mouth, glued my eyes half shut. My head felt like there was an angry blacksmith inside, trying to hammer his way out, and I wondered if my skull was broken. At least it made me forget the pain in my shoulder. I was freezing, too, but I was getting used to that.

They must have hidden Verity and me in the back of the buckboard when they left the fort. I caught the scent of violets where Verity had lain next to me; there was a greasy rope that had been used to tie her. I wondered if she knew I was alive. I was alone now, so either Verity was already dead or she was up front, on the seat with Granville and Haselmere. We must be on the road south to Fort Rice. It was the only road still open in this weather, except the one into Bismarck, and they would hardly be going there.

Then I heard Verity's voice, filtered through the heavy tarp. She sounded disillusioned, let down. "You asked me to marry you."

"Yes," replied Reed Granville, "and I meant it. But Hughes ruined everything. I love you, Verity, you must believe that."

"Really? Is that why you're going to kill me?"

"God knows, I tried to keep you out of this. Amos wanted to kill you when you started poking into the Redington story, but I thought we could make you give up."

"So you were the one who set those men on me?"

"I hoped they'd scare you off. Then Hughes came along. We kept trying to get rid of him, but we couldn't. If I had known what this scheme was going to cost me, I'd never have gotten involved with it."

"Why did you let them drag you into it in the first place? That's what I don't understand. What were you thinking of?"

I heard a short laugh that must have come from Haselmere, then Granville answered. "Nobody dragged me into it. It was my idea. Who do you think got Amos, here, appointed post trader? He didn't have those kinds of connections. My father knows Billy Belknap. He was a political contributor of his, back when we had money. I knew Belknap was corrupt—it's hardly a secret. Through my father, I got Belknap to put in a word to Orvil Grant about the post tradership at Fort Lincoln. Throw in Amos's thousand dollars, and it was a done deal. Belknap kicked out the last post trader for us. That's why I volunteered to be quartermaster, to help the reservation scheme along. It's extra work, but it paid off."

"How do you come to know an odious creature like Mr. Haselmere?"

"I've known Amos since the war. He was a sutler then, following the army. We conducted some mutually profitable business."

"Swindles, you mean?"

"Call it what you will. Then we ran into each other in

Bismarck and decided to work together again."

I knew that I should do something heroic, but the shotgun blow to my head had sapped my strength. All I could do was lay in pain and listen.

Verity was speaking again. "You've dishonored your uniform. You dishonored your Medal of Honor."

"Don't patronize me, Verity," Granville said. "I haven't dishonored anything. I earned that medal. I'll earn another if I get the chance. But I may never get that chance. I'm twenty-seven, and I don't even have the rank I had ten years ago. How do you think that feels? How will I make general at this rate? How will I amount to anything as a soldier? I'm like Custer—I wish the war hadn't ended. If it hadn't, I might have beaten his record as youngest general in the army. I felt alive during the war, Verity. I felt fulfilled. This, peacetime, is like . . . I don't know how to describe it. It's like running in place, playing soldier instead of being one. An Indian skirmish every couple years hardly breaks the monotony."

"So you became a thief out of boredom?"

"I did it for the money. I don't like being poor. I wasn't born that way; I don't intend to live that way. If I can't have rank, at least I want money to enjoy myself. Plus I have to support my parents, and that's damned hard on a first lieutenant's pay."

"You must know it can't continue."

"Why not? Peter Redington tried to interfere, and look what happened to him. The same with your friend Hughes. Once you're gone, there'll be no one who knows—or suspects—what we're doing. I just wish you hadn't gotten involved. Morgan and I killed Redington. I'd been planning it for a while, and the cold snap gave me the idea of tying it in with Doyle—bucking and gagging seemed like the kind of idiot stunt Doyle would pull. I left the club before Peter. I got Morgan, and we jumped Peter as he was going back to his quarters after the fight with Manley. We busted his head and carried him out on the prairie. Let him freeze to death—he deserved it.

"We didn't count on Doyle being a witness to what we'd done, but we had a good plan to cover ourselves. Having General Jack's detective show up made it even better. We had Sergeant Morgan to feed him information and keep an eye on him. When Morgan planted the watch in Doyle's mattress, that should have been the end of it. But Hughes had to keep nosing around."

Granville's voice had grown bitter; Verity's reply dripped with her old snooty superiority. "Private Doyle's information was enough to keep me on the story, no matter how many of your warnings I received. But if you hadn't set those two barbarians to frighten me off that night, Mr. Hughes might not have kept 'nosing around,' as you put it. Your guilt might have gone undetected. So what's happened is your own fault."

There was a long sigh, then Granville said, "In other words, if I hadn't loved you so much, I might not be forced to kill you now. Ironic, isn't it? You've broken my heart, Verity. Damn you. Damn myself."

"Stop being melodramatic," Verity told him.

"We're doing what has to be done, that's all," added Haselmere.

"What are you going to do with me?" Verity asked.

Haselmere replied. I could picture his oily grin as he spoke. "There's a deep ravine just up the road. We're going to shoot you and leave you there, along with your friend Hughes. Your bodies won't be found till spring, when the snow melts. If anybody recognizes you after the animals get done with you, they'll figure Indians killed you."

Granville said, "Look, Amos — maybe if she swore to keep quiet about this. We wouldn't have to — "

"Not going soft on me, are you, Reed?" growled Haselmere. "We agreed this was the only way."

"I know, but I don't want to do it. I'll still marry you, Verity. I'll give you money — anything you want. Just promise not to tell."

Haselmere said, "Damn you, Reed — "

"Oh, stop arguing," Verity said. "I won't swear to anything. Not to you. I'd rather die than lower myself that far. The only thing I'll swear to, is that, if you let me go, I'll head straight to the authorities. And as for marrying you, it may be a cliché, but I wouldn't marry you if you were the last man on earth."

There was a silence, then Granville's voice hardened. "Have it your way."

Soon afterwards, Haselmere said, "Here we are."

The buckboard jolted to a stop in the snow; I heard the foot brake creak. Verity said, "Before we do this, tell me one thing, Reed. Did you kill Sitting Bull?"

"Who?"

"Sitting Bull, my dog," Verity said, and now there were tears in her voice. "Were you the one that killed him?"

"I did it," Haselmere answered. "Reed didn't have the heart."

"I'll give him credit for something, then. I can almost understand your killing Lieutenant Redington, and me, and Mister Hughes — but a poor defenseless dog?"

"Not too defenseless," Haselmere said. "The damn

thing bit me."

Granville explained. "It was one last attempt to make you back off, to shock you into seeing how serious a situation you'd gotten into. But, like always, the more we tried to get you away from the story, the more time you spent with Hughes."

"All right," Haselmere said. "We've talked enough."

Granville said, "Get down, Verity. Don't fight. This is hard enough as it is."

"Don't worry, Reed. I wouldn't want you to have a crisis of conscience."

The buckboard's springs creaked as the three of them climbed down. I heard their footsteps mushing away in the snow.

It was now or never. I pushed aside the tarp. My head seemed to explode to five times its normal size with the effort, then contract and explode again. Blood-crusted skin cracked painfully as my eyes opened wide, taking in the steely gray daylight. I half rolled, half fell off the back of the buckboard, landing in the snow. I pushed myself up and lurched forward, running, stumbling, out of control, struggling to keep my balance.

The three of them had stopped at the side of the ravine. "I'll do it," Haselmere said. Granville turned away, but Verity refused to. She stood bolt upright, facing Haselmere, daring him. He shrugged and pointed his pistol at her forehead. He cocked it.

Verity and Granville saw me first; Haselmere, a half-second later. I must have made a sight, my face covered with blood. "Christ," Haselmere said, and he turned the pistol toward me. As he did, Verity snatched it from his hand. The cocked hammer fell and the pistol fired, but the bullet went into the ground. As Haselmere lunged to regain the weapon, Verity turned it, cocked, and fired again.

This was in the back of my eye as I came forward. My focus was on Granville turning toward me and the shotgun rising in his hands. The yawning double barrels looked like railroad tunnels. I went low. The shotgun exploded above my head; I felt its hot blast along my back. At the same time I took Granville in the stomach with my shoulder, knocking the air from him. We both sprawled in the snow. I recovered first, grabbing the shotgun and rising. Nearby, Haselmere rolled on the ground with a bullet in his side.

Verity stood beside me, holding the pistol, covering Granville and Haselmere. Good work," I told her.

"I can't believe you're alive," she said, staring at me wide eyed. "You had stopped breathing."

"I started again." My head was pounding like a thousand tom-toms; my shoulder felt like somebody had stuck a branding iron in it. The force of my charge had reopened both of my wounds, and the back of my jacket had been burned off by the shotgun blast. "I'm bleeding."

"You're always bleeding," Verity said.

On the ground, Granville shook his head and sat up. He saw Verity holding the pistol on him, and he swore. "Get up," I told him.

He did, and stood before us. He glared at me, then turned in supplication. "Verity —"

I swung the shotgun butt and hit him in the head as hard as I could. He dropped in the snow without a sound.

"I owed him that," I said.

"Is he dead?" Verity asked.

"I hope not. I want him to swing for what he's done."

CHAPTER 33

General Custer put the sword aside and held out his hand. "It seems I was wrong about you, Mister Hughes. Please accept my apologies."

"No apology needed, General," I replied.

We were in Custer's high-ceilinged library. Libby was there, along with Tom Custer, Keogh, and Lieutenant Cooke, with his dundreary whiskers. Major Reno, the post's highest ranking officer after Custer, had not been called. The late December sun had come out, and its pale light filtered through the window, highlighting drifting smoke from Keogh's pungent Havana cigar. Outside, bugles were blowing "Recall From Fatigue." Verity and I had brought the buckboard back to the fort, with Haselmere wounded and Reed Granville tied up next to him. We'd been arrested by the guard, but, fortunately for us, quick-witted young Jacky Sturgis was Officer of the Day. He'd listened to my story and taken us to Custer's residence instead of the guardhouse. Granville and Haselmere had been spirited through the back door to the ballroom, while Sturgis had escorted Verity and me to Custer's library.

The General had summoned his circle of advisors. The little group had stared at us—me, covered with blood, my uniform in shreds; Verity dressed as a soldier, her feet wrapped in strips from my overcoat. Verity had tried to clean my face by rubbing it with snow, but she had succeeded mainly in streaking the dried blood. My shoulder still hurt like hell, and I was so tired, I was almost out on my feet; but I had told them the story behind Lieutenant Redington's murder, and Verity vouched for its truth.

As I talked, Custer toyed with a huge sword that he'd captured in the war, swinging it back and forth. Everyone except Libby, who had total confidence in her husband, moved back, lest they have an arm or leg lopped off.

"Blast," Custer said after apologizing to me, "I wish I had a glass of Aldernay to calm my stomach. This is enough to drive a man back to hard liquor. That an officer in the United States Army—in this regiment—should have conspired to commit murder. And one of my best officers, to boot. My protégé. Why, it's monstrous, a disgrace to the uniform. I'll see the fellow court martialed. I'll see him hung. By Geoffrey, I've a mind to horse whip him as well."

"You can't, Autie," Libby said quietly.

All eyes turned toward her. "What?" said Custer. "I can't horse whip him?"

"You can't court martial him."

"Why the devil not?"

Libby put back her head and sighed. "Had Peter Redington's killer been an enlisted man, as we supposed, a court martial would have been the appropriate outcome. A certain number of enlisted men go bad, that's expected. Everyone knows there's rotten apples in the bunch. But an officer—a Medal of Honor winner? I am offended by Lieutenant Granville's actions as much as anyone, but if what he did is made public, it will be front page news in every paper in the country—Europe, as well. The scandal will reflect on you, Autie—you *are* the Seventh Cavalry. It will mean the end of your political career, possibly your military career, as well. Those jealous, mean-spirited men in Washington are always looking for a chance to undermine you. If it doesn't end your career, it will dog you forever. People will forget the great things you've accomplished. All they'll remember about you is that one of your officers murdered another."

Custer looked skeptical. "You're right, m'dear, as always. But I don't know. There's the question of my duty here . . . "

"Fiddlesticks. Your duty is to serve your country. How will throwing away your career accomplish that? Your country needs you too much to lose you over a sordid affair like this."

"Mm." Custer took a turn round the room, tugging at his walrus moustache with one hand, flexing the sword with the other. "What do you suggest?"

"I think that, for the good of the regiment—for the good of the service—Mr. Granville must be allowed to resign as quietly as possible."

Verity sprang to her feet. "Mrs. Custer! I must protest! The man is a murderer, he must be punished!"

Libby gave Verity a thin-lipped smile. "Army matters are best left to the army, my dear."

"You're not in the army. You're just the lieutenant-colonel's wife."

Every man in the room froze. In the stillness, I heard the mouse Diodorus digging in its ink well nest, as if seeking cover.

Libby Custer's benign, everyone's-favorite-aunt look had vanished, replaced by a set jaw and eyes that would have lowered the temperature of hell. Before she could say anything, Custer intervened. "Libby's right, Miss Winslow. I appreciate your concern, but you'll please allow those familiar with the consequences to sort this out."

"Consequences?" I interjected. "Isn't justice a consequence? Isn't that why I was hired?"

"Life is complicated, Mister Hughes," Libby explained patiently, the favorite aunt again, talking to a child. "Sometimes we must compromise."

Leaning against the fireplace mantel, Myles Keogh took the cigar from his mouth and cleared his throat. "If I may be permitted to make a suggestion?"

"Go ahead," Custer said.

"The regiment is short of officers. Approximately one-fourth are on detached duty of one kind or other, and we're not likely to get many back before the campaign starts. If any become casualties, we're going to have companies commanded by sergeants. Why not let Granville go on the campaign with his troop? We can use a man with his experience. He can resign when we come back." He paused. "Who knows—he may even die a glorious death, and save us all a lot of trouble."

Custer pursed his lips. He looked at Libby, who nodded.

"Very well," Custer said. "But Amos Haselmere must resign as post trader immediately—if he survives his wound." Libby nodded again, approving. Verity and I stared at each other. Verity was even angrier than I was, because she had been betrayed twice—once by the man she loved, now by Custer.

Custer had begun pacing again, holding the sword behind his back. He looked toward his friends, a glint in his eye. "So, Billy Belknap has been selling out the Indians, eh? Taking profits from the post traders? By Geoffrey, I've wanted to get the goods on that fellow for a long time. I'll have his scalp, or I'm Jeff Davis. The Democrats will owe me."

"You can run for president as 'The Man to Clean up Washington,'" said Brother Tom.

Custer turned to me once more. "Hughes, I like you. You're a man who gets things done. The kind of man I want with me. Tell you what. Stay in the army, and I'll make you a sergeant. You can sew on the stripes when you leave this room. I know you don't get on with Myles, here, so you won't have to stay in his troop. Pick any troop you like. I'm sure Jimmy Calhoun would love to have you. What do you say?"

"Thanks, General, but I had my fill of soldiering during the war. Besides, I have to look for my sister. I can't wait five years."

"Come on the spring campaign as a civilian scout, then. I'll pay you top dollar—a hundred and fifty a month. We're going to make history out there. Bags of glory for everyone. Come along and be part of it."

I thought the offer over. "I admit, I'm tempted. You're right about history being made, and there's a piece of me that wants to be there to see it, to take part in it. But I never found any glory in killing Indians just for the sake of doing it, and that's what this little trip is going to be about. I never thought I'd agree with Miss Winslow, but this isn't going to be a war, it's extermination. I'll have to pass."

Custer couldn't believe he'd been turned down. His keen blue eyes went blank, as if I had suddenly ceased to exist for him, and he turned away from me. He replaced the sword in its scabbard of red Moroccan leather, and hung it on the wall. "Libby, gentlemen—it's time for us to speak to Mister Granville."

Without a word to Verity or me, he held the door open for Libby, and the little group filed out of the room, save for Lieutenant Cooke, who stayed behind to pay me the additional ten dollars I had coming.

"Can I say goodbye to my friends?" I asked him.

"Better not. There's liable to be bad blood when they find out you were a detective."

I understood, and nodded. "Wish them luck for me."

"I will." Cooke stuck out his hand. "Goodbye, Hughes. Sorry you're going to miss the big show."

"Goodbye, Lieutenant."

Cooke turned and bowed. "Miss Winslow, good day to you."

"Lieutenant," said Verity, with a barely perceptible nod of the head.

Verity and I left Custer's house. We didn't wait for the post ambulance to take us to the river, but walked, drawing stares as we skirted the parade ground. Men recognized me and pointed, until their sergeants recalled them to their duties.

Whitey Tarr was on guard at the fort's main gate. "Right about you all along, weren't I, Pretty Boy?" he said. "You're a Pinkerton, or some such." Standing at parade rest, head pointed rigidly forward, he spit out the side of his mouth at me. "Should've slit your throat when I had the chance."

I laughed. "It was nice knowing you, too, Whitey."

Verity and I walked down the road to Bismarck. We kept to the side, preferring to negotiate the snow rather than flounder in the semi-frozen mud of the road. Verity was filled with righteous outrage at what had just taken place. My own outrage was tempered by experience; I had seen similar things happen too many times before. It was the way the world worked.

"What are you going to do now?" I asked Verity.

"Work on my story, of course. Miss Holier-Than-Thou may think she can hush up this affair, but she hasn't reckoned with the power of the press. Oh, no. When I'm done, the whole country will know how Peter Redington died—and why. This story will make my career." She looked over at me. "What about you? What are you going to do?"

"The first thing I'm going to do is get a good meal and a night's sleep."

"And after that?"

"After that, I figure on heading south, to New Mexico."

"To look for your sister?"

I nodded. "There's still a few Comancheros left out there. I want to talk to them."

"Well, good luck. Try not to bleed too much."

"I'll do my best."

"Who knows—maybe we'll work together again one day."

My mind boggled at the thought, but I answered politely. "Stranger things have happened."

Suddenly she stood on tiptoe and kissed my cheek.

"What was that for?" I said.

"I don't know. It just seemed like the right thing to do."

She hooked her arm through mine, and we walked down to the frozen river. Behind us, on the parade ground, the regimental band was practicing. They were playing "Garry Owen."

EPILOGUE

It's strange, but the most famous battle in American history was an Indian skirmish. More ink has been spilled over the Little Big Horn than blood was shed there, and since I saw the Seventh Cavalry from a unique perspective, I guess I should spill my share.

In my opinion, there was no other officer in the Seventh, from the much-maligned Reno to greenhorn Jacky Sturgis, who would have handled the regiment as badly as Custer did on that fateful June Sunday. Most of the enlisted men would have handled it better. Custer violated every precept of warfare. He took largely untrained men and horses, pushed them to the limits of their endurance on a grueling two-day march, then threw them piecemeal against the greatest force of Indians ever assembled on the North American continent, with no knowledge of the terrain and no idea of the enemy's numbers or dispositions. It was the same "strategy" he always employed, and on that day it caught up with him. Custer's luck ran out.

There was an otherworldly quality about the Seventh Cavalry. It was as if the regiment only existed to assist its lieutenant-colonel in his mythic quest for glory. The fortunes of men like Peaches and Dick Daring and Two Bit were nothing to Custer except as they brought him closer to his Holy Grail. Basking in his aura was supposed to be reward enough for them. I knew those men. They were as brave as any who ever served the United States.

They didn't want to die, but they realized there was a chance they would have to, and it was a chance they were willing to take. All they asked was a good reason why and halfway competent leadership. They didn't enlist to immortalize the name of a man who cared nothing about them.

They deserved better than that.

One question remains about Custer's performance at the Little Big Horn—was he under the added pressure of achieving a great victory in order to salvage his career? He had gone to Washington in the early months of 1876. Armed with the information I had supplied him, he brought down Secretary of War Belknap, first writing an "anonymous" letter to the *New York Herald*, then testifying about Belknap's corruption in Congress, forcing Belknap to resign. But in so doing he incurred the wrath of Belknap's patron, President Grant, who removed him from his command. At one point, Custer reportedly got on his knees and in tears begged General Terry to intercede for his reinstatement. Terry did, with results that are known to all. But Custer's reputation, and his career, had been damaged.

Perhaps Custer hoped to use the Belknap affair to his benefit. He had incurred a deal of sympathy, especially in Democratic Party circles, because of the way Grant treated him. Though the campaign's start was delayed from February until May, Custer may have believed he still had just enough time to win a great victory and have the news relayed to the Democratic convention, as the delegates were preparing to select their presidential nominee. Either way, did the events I set in motion cause him to be even more reckless than usual on that day in 1876? We'll never know, but I'll always wonder . . .

* * *

Verity Winslow wrote her story, but the Custers denied everything in it. It was never published, and Verity lost her job at the *Tribune* because of it. The place she coveted on the Big Horn expedition was taken by Mark Kellogg.

Libby Custer devoted the rest of her life to promoting the myth of her husband's saintliness, heroism, and military genius, suppressing negative stories about his life—and death. Supposedly many officers would not talk—or altered their testimony—about the Little Big Horn and the events leading to it for fear of incurring her wrath.

And Reed Granville? His troop wasn't involved in the massacre. He fought on Reno Hill with the rest of the regiment, and there he died. "Killed by hostile fire" was the official cause, but there were rumors that he was shot in the back by one of his own men.

Oh, and remember Mrs. Nash, the Seventh Cavalry's "super laundress?" A year after the Little Big Horn, she suddenly took sick and died. As she was being laid out for burial, it was discovered that the "Aztec princess" had in reality been—a man.

APPENDIX

Excerpt from the *Bismarck Tribune* Extra. Bismarck, D.T. July 6, 1876. A partial list of those killed at the Little Big Horn.

KILLED
Field and Staff. George A. Custer. Brevt. Major General.
W.W. Cook. Brevt. Lt.-Colonel.
Lord. Asst. Surgeon. J.M. DeWolf. Acting Asst. Surgeon

A.C. Staff. W.W. Sharrow. Sarg.-Major.

C. .	T.W. Custer	Brevt. Lt.-Col.
C.	Finley	Sergt.
C.	Windham	Privt.

| E. | E. Sturgis | 2d Lt. |

The body of Lt. Sturgis was not found, but it is reasonably certain that he was killed.

| L. | James Calhoun | 1st Lt. |

I.	M.W. Keogh	Col.
I.	J.E. Porter—the body of Lt. Porter was not found, but it is reasonably certain he was killed.	
I.	F.E. Varden	1st Sergt.
I.	J. Bustard	Sergt.
I.	John Wild	Corpl.
I.	G.C. Morris	"
I.	S.T. Staples	"
I.	J.M. Gucker	"
I.	J. Patton	Trptr.
I.	H.A. Baily	Blacksmith

232

I.	J.E. Broadhurst	Privt.
I.	J. Barry	"
I.	J. Conners	"
I.	T.P. Downing	"
I.	Mason	"
I.	Blorm	"
I.	Meyer	"
I.	McElroy	Trptr
I.	Mooney	"
I.	Baker	Privt.
I.	Boyle	"
I.	Bauth	"
I.	Conner	"
I.	Daring	"
I.	Davis	"
I.	Farrell	"
I.	Hiley	"
I.	Huber	"
I.	Hime	"
I.	Henderson	"
I.	Henderson	"
I.	Leddisson	"
I.	O'Conner	"
I.	Rood	"
I.	Reese	"
I.	Smith 1st	"
I.	Smith 2nd	"
I.	Smith 3rd	"
I.	Stella	"
I.	Stafford	"
I.	Schoole	"
I.	Smallwood	"
I.	Tarr	"
I.	Vaugant	"
I.	Walker	"
I.	Bragew	"

F.	G.W. Yates	Capt.
F.	W.Van Riley	2d Lt.
F.	Vickory	Sergt.
F.	Ruddew	Privt.
F.	E.C. Driscoll	"

Mark Kellogg .... Civilian

THE END

About the Author

Robert Broomall is the author of a number of published novels. Besides writing, his chief interests are travel and history, especially military history, the Old West, and the Middle Ages. He also likes to cook, much to the dismay of those who have to eat what he prepares.

Amazon author page: **https://www.amazon.com/author/ robertbroomall**

Facebook page:
https://www.facebook.com/robertbroomall.author

Connect with Bob: **robertbroomall@gmail.com**

Made in the USA
Monee, IL
24 August 2022

12400037R00134